SUSANNAH HART
Nobody's Baby

Silhouette Desire

Published by Silhouette Books New York

America's Publisher of Contemporary Romance

SILHOUETTE BOOKS, a Simon & Schuster Division of
GULF & WESTERN CORPORATION
1230 Avenue of the Americas, New York, N.Y. 10020

ISBN: 0-671-47018-3

First Silhouette Books printing June, 1983

10 9 8 7 6 5 4 3 2 1

America's Publisher of Contemporary Romance

Printed in the U.S.A.

"What Else Do You Want from Me?"

"This, for a start." He narrowed the gap between her lips and his and brushed her mouth with the gentlest of kisses. Faith's pulse raced as Nick repeated the act, each kiss slowly building her hunger for the full possession of his mouth. Her hands slipped up around his neck.

"Nick—" she said, in an odd voice. He brushed a finger across her parted lips.

"First, promise."

"Anything."

"Go to the police and swear out a complaint against that boy. I'll give you the case number and the officer's name."

Faith turned numb. Go to the police. Press charges. Was his touch nothing but sweet manipulation to persuade her . . . ?

SUSANNAH HART

is an accomplished playwright, poet and journalist who recently left the staff of a national magazine to indulge her lifelong passion for writing love stories. She lives in New York City with her husband and infant son. *Nobody's Baby* is her first Desire.

Dear Reader:

Silhouette has always tried to give you exactly what you want. When you asked for increased realism, deeper characterization and greater length, we brought you Silhouette Special Editions. When you asked for increased sensuality, we brought you Silhouette Desire. Now you ask for books with the length and depth of Special Editions, the sensuality of Desire, but with something else besides, something that no one else offers. Now we bring you SILHOUETTE INTIMATE MOMENTS, true romance novels, longer than the usual, with all the depth that length requires. More sensuous than the usual, with characters whose maturity matches that sensuality. Books with the ingredient no one else has tapped: excitement.

There is an electricity between two people in love that makes everything they do magic, larger than life—and this is what we bring you in SILHOUETTE INTIMATE MOMENTS. Look for them wherever you buy books.

These books are for the woman who wants more than she has ever had before. These books are for you. As always, we look forward to your comments and suggestions. You can write to me at the address below:

Karen Solem
Editor-in-Chief
Silhouette Books
P.O. Box 769
New York, N.Y. 10019

1

Too dangerous. Much too risky," Faith Daniels muttered as the cab stopped for a light at the corner of Sixtieth and Fifth Avenue. "Why did I ever say I'd go?"

Her friend looked across at Faith's earnest face, now drawn with worry. "We've been through this a hundred times."

"I know." Faith smiled in apology. "I'm sorry, Bonnie. But since you're the only person who knows about this—"

"That's the price you pay when you have a secret life, kiddo. Shortage of confidants."

"You make it sound so glamorous." Faith sighed. "If only—"

"The meter's runnin', girls," announced the cabbie in his broad Brooklyn accent. "Do I park it or what?"

"Just pull up in front of the Plaza," Bonnie said.

"The Plaza, is it? For a wedding, maybe? I couldn't help noticing your dress, miss."

"The Mystery Writers of America Banquet," Bonnie said. "My friend's been nominated for an Edgar."

"Shh!" said Faith.

"You're kidding!" said the cabbie. "Isn't that grand, now? What's an Edgar?"

"An award for mystery writing," Faith said. "Named for Edgar Allan Poe."

"And you're getting one."

"I've only been nominated—" Faith said.

"Nominated, shnominated. It's an honor, just the same."

"Exactly my point." Bonnie's brown curls bobbed up and down. "You've got to go."

"What if someone recognizes me?" Faith protested. "I've got this funny feeling—"

"Who's going to recognize you?" Bonnie asked. "You know nobody from the Foundation will come within miles of the Plaza. They might be contaminated by wealth." Her dramatic shudder drew a laugh from Faith. "Anyway, you don't look a bit like your everyday self, believe me."

"Still . . ." Faith wasn't convinced. True, her fair hair hung long and loose on her shoulders instead of pulled back in its accustomed French twist. Her gown was ankle-length pale blue silk, its daring off-the-shoulder bodice highlighted by an antique brooch of diamonds and stunning aquamarines. This one dress had cost almost as much as her entire office wardrobe. But these were mere camoflaugings; beneath the finery, she was still plain Faith Daniels, who had never in her twenty-three years presented herself at a public function without her strict and autocratic aunt by her side.

"Wait. Take this." Faith slipped off her diamond ring and dropped it into Bonnie's hand.

"Your ring? Why?"

"It's a Clinton family heirloom," Faith replied nervously. "Somebody might recognize it."

Bonnie laughed and told Faith her paranoia was getting out of hand. "Do you really expect to find one of Harald's relatives skulking around tonight? Or are the Clinton family jewels that famous?"

Faith sighed. "You never know—with my luck, they will be. Here—maybe you'd better take these, too. Just to be on the safe side." Faith removed her trim tortoiseshell glasses and gave them to Bonnie. Faith's eyes, suddenly revealed, were huge, blue and luminous.

"Are you sure? Disguise is all well and good, but we can't have the nominee walk into walls."

"I'll manage." The cab rolled to a stop in front of the imposing façade of the Plaza Hotel. Faith swallowed hard and looked up at the rounded towers, the flags bathed in a misty twilight.

"Well, miss?"

"Shoot." Faith's smile was rueful. "If I don't go, I'll spend the rest of my life wondering what I missed." She took a deep breath and pushed the door open. "But I'm tempting fate."

"Fate was meant to be tempted," Bonnie called as the cab sped away.

Faith's resolve wavered when she approached the ballroom where the banquet was to take place. Amid the clusters of noisy, party-minded people she felt out of place—small, adrift, alone—and in danger.

"Waiting for someone?"

Faith looked up. The speaker was a tall, dark-haired man with a compassionate face. His faint accent and superbly tailored tweeds allowed Faith to pinpoint his place of birth with an accuracy Henry Higgins would have envied.

"No." Faith's throat was so dry her voice cracked.

"You don't mean you're alone, by any chance? What luck! My wife Alicia was delayed in London—one of the boys fell out of a tree and broke his leg, of all the fool things, and I'm by myself."

He smiled at Faith as if she were a long-lost friend. "I prayed I could find someone to share my table, but I never dreamed the gods would come through quite so handsomely." He held out his hand. "I'm Ken Powell, by the way."

"I know," Faith said. She'd seen his photo many times, beaming out from the jackets of his books. His current bestseller was nominated for best mystery novel of the year. "You're up for the big one tonight, aren't you? Good luck."

"Thanks." Ken grinned. "I'm trying my best to look modest, but Alicia says I'm hopeless. This is the third time round for me, and I haven't won yet."

"Third time's a charm, they say. I'm sure you'll win. *Come Hell or High Water* is a marvelous book."

"So beautiful and brilliant, too," he murmured. "I insist that you join me for dinner."

Faith hesitated. She would love to talk to Ken Powell, and she would be far less tense with his company. But she couldn't take the risk.

"I'd love to," she lied, "but I was just on my way out."

"Really?"

"Yes. I-I just stopped by for a drink."

"In that dress?" Ken stared at her gown. "You're dressed to kill, my dear, and here's a roomful of men ripe for slaughter."

Faith colored. "I must go." She walked straight to the elevators and pressed the "down" button.

"I'm not making a pass at you," came Ken's lazy voice from behind her.

"I didn't think you were," Faith replied stiffly.

"Of course you did, and quite right, too. If I were single . . ." He shrugged. "I'd like your company, that's all. What do you say?"

Faith hesitated. "Well . . ."

"You do want to go in, don't you?"

Faith bit her lip. She did—she couldn't deny it. "Oh, all right," she said.

"Now there's an enthusiastic response." Ken took her elbow and guided her into the ballroom. "You'd better watch building my ego like that, girl, or I'll be even more conceited than I am now."

Faith's eyes widened as they entered the room. "How beautiful," she whispered. Even with her blurred vision, she saw the crystal chandeliers, the velvet-backed chairs tucked against small round tables, the bright parrot tulips and anemones that beckoned from every tabletop.

This is a palace, Faith thought. Dozens of low white candles in glass holders cast circles of flickering light about the room. She had never seen any place so romantic.

"Shall we find a table for two?" Ken asked.

"Please," Faith said.

"By the way, I can't go on calling you 'girl' all night. Do you have a name, or are you a woman of mystery?"

"Of course I have a name," Faith replied, and then stopped short. For tonight she had another name; she'd better remember that.

She hesitated only a moment. "I'm Fanny Duvall." The name sounded exotic on her tongue, full of provocative possibilities.

"Fanny Duvall," Ken repeated, and his brow furrowed as if trying to recall an elusive fact. "Wait—you're not *Blood Poisoning?*"

Faith's quick-to-flush cheeks glowed with pleasure as she admitted she was.

"Why, congratulations, you sly minx," Ken said. "You're nominated too, aren't you?"

"For best *first* novel," she emphasized. "Not quite the same league as you."

"My first novel wouldn't have won a booby prize," Ken said dryly. "Well, no wonder you had such a case of jitters at the door. Hell on the old nerves, isn't it?"

"You've no idea," Faith said fervently. "I wasn't prepared for all this."

Her gesture took in the dais, where microphones sprouted from the podium; the eight-piece orchestra tuning up across the room; and the scores of people milling around, all drinking, smoking, and talking at the top of their voices. She was glad to follow Ken to a small table on the fringe of the crowd.

"First time, huh?" Ken pulled out her chair and she sat. "It's rather like sex—waiting for it to happen is the worst part."

"You're so comforting."

"I do my best." He smiled, then sat opposite Faith and signaled a waiter who carried a tray of champagne glasses. The waiter placed goblets before them. "To our mutual success."

"May we live happily ever after," Faith said, and sipped the champagne cautiously.

"Don't look so nervous. You know you'll win."

"I know no such thing," she protested. "Anyway that's presumptuous, to expect to win on your first time out. I'm prepared to suffer plenty before I get rewarded."

"That's a harsh view," he commented.

"I've led a harsh life." Faith's words slipped out automatically.

"I believe you have." Ken looked at her, curiosity warring with concern on his mobile face. "Care to talk about it?"

"Not tonight." Tonight she was Fanny Duvall, who had no unhappy past to regret. She gave Ken her brightest smile and concentrated on turning the conversation to less embarrassing channels. "Tell me what you're working on now."

He did. As if he sensed her anxiety, Ken diverted Faith with funny and libelous accounts of the London publishing world. His stories kept her entranced from the clear green-turtle soup through the chicken and mushrooms bordelaise. Eventually, Faith relaxed enough to respond with some stories of her own. She was shocked when Ken interrupted her and pointed to movement behind her back.

"I say, we've made the big time. Look there."

Faith twisted in her velvet-backed chair and squinted, expecting to see yet another celebrity author. What she saw made a lump of chicken lodge in her throat. Faith choked, and struggled to swallow.

"Is that a television crew, for heaven's sake?"

"It is indeed."

"Oh, no! Why the devil are they here?"

"The Edgars are news, my dear," Ken replied. "Marginal, in my opinion, but an award is an award is an award."

Faith gulped down some water and rose, clutching her purse. "I've got to get out of here."

"Fanny! Sit down. Are you ill? You can't leave now—they're almost ready to start the presentation."

"You don't understand," Faith whispered. "I didn't know there'd be any television coverage."

Ken frowned. "What difference does that make?"

Life or death, Faith thought grimly. Safety or peril. "Please don't ask me any questions," she begged. "Just help me to get out of here. Now." She darted a glance over her shoulder, looking for the fastest route to the hallway. "I've got to hurry—"

"You're not leaving without telling me why," Ken argued. "Have I been such a monster?"

"No. Not at all. It's not you, it's just—" She stammered, unable to continue.

"What's this all about?" Ken half rose from his chair and put a restraining hand on her arm; Faith realized he would follow her if she attempted to leave.

"I can't be seen on camera," Faith blurted desperately. "Now will you please let me go before it's too late?"

Ken's eyes widened; his jaw dropped in delighted surprise. "Fanny Duvall, you beautiful fraud. Now I see. You're leading a double life!"

That was the truth; she couldn't deny it. She sat, tongue-tied, looking guilty, as the waiter materialized and removed the dinner plates. Faith twisted her hands in her lap, and tried to think of a plausible story to tell Ken. Stupid of her not to have planned a cover story beforehand, and he would be hard to fool, with his background. Just her luck.

The waiter placed goblets of strawberry mousse at their places and vanished. Faith met Ken's eyes. "I'm right, aren't I?" he demanded.

Weakly, she nodded.

"And if you're seen on television as Fanny Duvall, novelist, your cover as whatever it is you really are will be blown sky-high?"

Faith nodded again.

"You are in a bit of a pickle, aren't you?"

"That's the understatement of the year."

Ken whistled and looked at her in frank admiration. Faith realized that she had been holding her breath—as if Ken might jump to his feet and announce he'd found an impostor—and she let the pent-up air out in a gush.

"Suppose—now don't jump out of your skin, Fanny— you do get on television and somebody recognizes you. How bad would that be?"

"All things considered, I'd rather be dead."

"That bad?" Faith lifted bleak blue eyes to his curious brown ones. Ken's hand reached across the table and covered hers. "I'm sorry," he said kindly. "I didn't mean to take your problem lightly."

"Don't apologize," Faith said. "How could you have known? I only hope I haven't ruined your evening . . ."

"Ruined it? Nonsense! Couldn't be better." He leaned forward. "I thrive on this, you know. Challenge for the old brain cells. We'll get you out safe and sound, never you worry."

"I shouldn't have come," Faith mourned. "I had a feeling something like this would happen. But I couldn't stay away."

"Like a moth to the flame," Ken said softly.

"I know, you think it's pure conceit. That I came because I was flattered and wanted to win. But the award doesn't matter to me. Truly. All I wanted was to be here, to see if I belonged." Faith's voice became nearly inaudible as she struggled to articulate her deepest need. "I've never really belonged anywhere since my parents died, and I thought that maybe here I'd feel—" She stopped, her throat constricted in pain.

"Never you worry," Ken said. He patted her hand. "Now let me get this clear. It can't be known that you, whoever you really are, and Fanny Duvall are the same person."

Faith nodded.

"Why not—if all Fanny Duvall has done is write a book? I assume that's all she's done . . . ?"

"It's my family. And my job." Faith sighed. "They'd object to the book. Find it too . . . spicy."

"God save us. You're a nun."

"Close," Faith said, laughing. "Very close."

"You don't work for one of those pressure groups— clean up the media and so forth?"

"Not directly, no, but I might as well." Faith saw the puzzled look in Ken's eyes and decided that she could trust him with a bit more information. "I work for a charitable foundation that raises funds for projects in poor neighborhoods. Community self-help. We're non-sectarian, but we work hand-in-hand with all the large religious charities, and our—oh, I guess you'd call it 'corporate image'—has to be above reproach."

"Including your personal life?" Ken asked. "No drinking, no smoking, no swearing, no racy books? What are you, the minister's wife?"

"Worse," Faith groaned. "I'm the founder's daughter. My father was killed in Mississippi during a civil rights crusade almost twenty years ago, but the Foundation has survived. Dad's sister runs it now; we try to carry on his work. . . ."

"Holy smoke," Ken said, "and I bet everyone has strong ideas about what the founder's baby daughter should do with her life."

"Especially what she *shouldn't* do," Faith said. She poked a spoon into her strawberry mousse and savagely mashed it to a pink liquid.

"And the Foundation wouldn't appreciate *Blood Poisoning?*"

"Are you kidding?" Faith demanded. "All that sex and violence?"

"My dear, I once wrote a book about a rapist, but that doesn't make me Jack the Ripper."

"Tell that to my Aunt Prue."

"She's rather strict, is she?"

Prudence Daniels could redefine the term "strict," but family loyalty would not permit Faith to say so. "Let's say tolerance is not her long suit."

"And she's the head of the Foundation?"

"And my only family. My dad's sister. Also my boss."

"A triple whammy."

"Laugh if you like," Faith said grimly, "but this is life-and-death for me. Aunt Prue's called the shots for me ever since my father died, and I've never dared cross her."

"You did once," he pointed out. "You wrote the book."

"Just for fun. I was still in college then. I never dreamed I could get *Blood Poisoning* published."

"But you tried, and now look where you are." Ken gestured at their opulent surroundings. "You're going to hell in a handbasket. Next thing you know you'll be leaving the family business to write full-time."

"Don't I wish!"

"Wishing will make it so," Ken murmured.

Faith gulped down a mouthful of coffee, her eyes lowered to hide the sudden mist of tears. He had stumbled on her dream. Faith longed to write as a career, instead of an hour snatched here and there, but how could she leave the Foundation?

"Lincoln freed the slaves, Fanny," Ken said, as if he guessed her thoughts. "You know you write well enough to support yourself, so why not cut loose?"

"Oh, the problem isn't money. That's not what scares me."

"What, then? Deserting your father's memory? You're hardly the first kid to want out of the family business."

"If it were only so simple," Faith said wistfully.

"Try and see," Ken urged. "If the guilt of leaving is too much for you to handle, you can always go back to the Foundation."

"But I believe in the Foundation's work. I'm needed there. And I'm loyal to my father's memory."

"Still, you have to come out of the closet someday."

"Someday," Faith admitted, "but not tonight. I'm not ready."

"Are we ever ready? *Blood Poisoning* could win, you

know. Wouldn't that be great publicity for the Foundation?"

"No!" she cried. "I'd never live it down!"

"Live it down? Your aunt won't think you've murdered half a dozen people as a background exercise, will she?"

"No, but Prue'll say I must have . . ."

"Must have what?"

Her voice dropped. "Slept with a lot of men as background for the love story."

"Fanny, child, one good man would be enough."

Faith blushed and turned away to hide her confusion. The whole subject of sex embarrassed her. Even now, at twenty-three, past her teenage awkwardness and possessed of a devastatingly eligible fiancé, she still found sex disappointing. She had concluded, sadly, that she was one of those women who was simply incapable of feeling passion. . . .

Then she saw him.

The man cut a swath through the tables at the back of the room like Moses parting the Red Sea. Something about his masterful gait rang a bell in her memory. Faith's eyes narrowed to make out his face as he came closer.

She saw dark hair, full and waving over a high forehead, deep-set eyes over prominent cheekbones, a sharp chin, a narrow, sensual mouth. He wore his clothes with a casual elegance that took their perfection for granted. He would be a dangerously attractive man, Faith thought, even without the vivid intelligence that shone through his every expression, his every movement. With it, he was formidable.

Faith's hand tightened convulsively on Ken's. "Look!"

"What the devil?" Ken whipped his head around to follow the path of her eyes.

"It's Nick Justin," Faith whispered, "and he's looking right at us."

"Nick Justin? Where?" Even the Englishman didn't have to ask who Nick Justin was. Justin's brand of hard-hitting television journalism was famous the world over.

"Quiet," Faith begged. "Can't you see he's staring?" She tipped her long hair forward to hide her face.

"So he is," Ken said. "Well, well. I wonder what we've done to hit the big time? I wouldn't have thought the MWA could summon up enough corruption to interest the likes of Nick Justin." He pinched her hand. "Ease up, Fanny, you look paralyzed with fright."

"I've got to get out of here. I'm sure he's recognized you and in ten seconds he'll be here to interview you."

"Me? Guess again," Ken said dryly. "Give the man some credit. He wouldn't be worth his salary if he couldn't track down the most beautiful woman in the room."

"Oh, my God," Faith breathed. Nick Justin had turned and was looking full in her eyes from a distance not fifteen feet away. She felt like a doe looking down the barrel of a determined hunter's rifle.

"That's enough. I'm leaving," she announced, when Justin at last moved on. She pushed her chair back.

"You can't."

"Want to bet?"

"The awards are starting. Do you want to look even more suspicious?"

"You could accept for me, if I win. Say I've been taken ill."

"And do you think that would fool Nick Justin?" Ken demanded. "You'd only convince him you had something terrible to hide." Ken's voice was earnest. "You write mysteries. You know that flight connotes guilt."

"I don't care what he thinks as long as I get out of here."

"Justin, your aunt—you can always find someone to be scared of. They'll be glad to run your life for you if you can't manage it yourself."

"That's not fair."

"Fair doesn't enter into it. You wanted to know if you belonged here. We'll find out, won't we? You can brazen it out like a grownup, or you can run away."

Ken's derision wounded her. Faith was ashamed of her fear, but it was there all the same. Her instinct to run from danger warred with her desire to be brave; mingled with them was natural suspense about whether she would win the Edgar. Faith's head throbbed with confusion. Only one thought was predominant: if she ran like a scared rabbit she would be diminished, not only in Ken's eyes, but, more significantly, in her own.

She had to stay.

Faith settled back in her chair. "That's my girl," Ken said. He slid his chair around the edge of the table so that he was next to her and slipped a protective arm around her. "Looks like they're ready to go."

A man stepped up to the microphone on the dais and began to read a welcoming address.

"I don't care what you say," Faith muttered. "I can't go up there and face those cameras."

"Look on the bright side," Ken teased. "Maybe you'll lose."

Faith laughed in spite of herself. Indeed, she thought wryly, losing would be the best thing that could happen to her. Nick Justin wouldn't be interested in a loser. . . .

But she won.

When her name was announced, Faith was convinced it was a trick of her hearing. She remained frozen in her seat, lest she jump up and call attention to her foolishness. Only when Ken grabbed her, kissed her, impelled her forward, did she know it must be true: *Blood Poisoning* had won. Faith staggered to the dais, conscious only of the heat and the pounding in her ears. She accepted the ceramic bust of Poe with shaking hands, somehow spoke the proper words in a voice that sounded foreign to her ears.

Faith couldn't see much—without her glasses and with the television lights in her eyes—but she saw Nick Justin. Of course, he would be there, front and center, watching. His intense eyes stripped right through her. That lean and hungry look, she thought. What was the warning that went with it? *Such men are dangerous.* . . .

Faith's skin prickled with alarm. She couldn't step down from the dais fast enough.

She heard the applause then, waves of it, rushing over her. She looked down at the bust in her arms. The Edgar was real, it was hers. She let out a whoop of joy and cradled the bust like a baby and felt her way back to her table through tear-blurred eyes.

Faith set the bust on the table and collapsed into her seat. Ken Powell's arm came around her.

"You wouldn't have wanted to miss this, would you?" He grinned at her with paternal pride.

"Blood Poisoning . . ." She hesitated on the brink of a shy smile. "It's really good, isn't it?"

"Of course, you nitwit. Didn't you know?"

"Not until now," she whispered. "Not for sure."

"Be sure," he said. Faith felt a surge of happiness that swelled to a warm tide when she heard Ken's name called as winner in the last category, for best mystery novel of the year. His unbounded joy in his victory freed a restraint in her—she could celebrate Ken's victory with an unself-conscious delight she could never feel about her own efforts. But when he returned, dumped his Edgar down on the table, seized Faith and kissed her full on the lips, she blushed furiously and wriggled with embarrassment.

"I won," he said, as if in explanation.

"No kidding." Faith smoothed back her hair nervously and managed a smile. "I'm so happy for you."

"Thanks, Fanny. I've waited years for this."

Fanny. The alias brought Faith's deception back to her mind, reminding her of the danger of discovery. She had had her marvelous evening; now it was time for Fanny Duvall to disappear forever.

As she gathered up her purse and pushed back her chair, she felt Ken Powell's arm lock around her.

"Wait. Where're you going?"

"Home, remember?" There was a new edge of anxiety in Faith's voice. "And high time."

"You can't leave before you dance with me," Ken said. "We're winners. We have to celebrate, that's part of the bargain."

"Was not," Faith protested, her voice rising. "Have a heart, Ken, you know what a fix I'm in—"

"What fix is that, Miss Duvall?"

The voice froze Faith's breathing; it was a voice she knew by heart from hundreds of Tuesday evenings she'd spent watching *Newsview.* Faith felt a violent urge to flee. She would not have been the first to run from the onslaught of Nick Justin and his cameras. But instead she took a deep breath and pressed closer to Ken's side.

"Brazen it out," Ken had advised. Well, she would. She tossed her blond hair, and hoped Bonnie was right when she said Faith looked vastly different from her everyday self.

"Hello, Nick," Ken said, with a passable imitation of a smile. "Good to see you again."

"You, too. And Alicia?"

"Stayed behind in London. With the kids."

"I see." Justin's granite voice implied he saw a lot more than there was to see. He looked from Ken to Faith with barely veiled suspicion. Faith prickled with defiance.

"I believe congratulations are in order," Nick Justin went on, with a conventional politeness Faith didn't trust for a minute. "For both of you—if this is the mysterious Fanny Duvall?"

"Hardly mysterious," Faith replied. She made her voice as low and husky as possible and hoped that would disguise her nervousness. "But certainly Fanny Duvall."

She met Justin's eyes then. They weren't brown, as she had always thought, but hazel, flecked with vivid green.

"Then I congratulate you," he said, "on your victory." He almost smiled. Faith felt a sudden peculiar sensation in her stomach, as if she'd dropped several hundred feet in an instant.

"Thank you," she murmured at last.

"Surprised to see you here, Nick," Ken said. "I'd have thought we writers far too tame to intrigue the likes of you."

"On the contrary," Nick Justin said. "I've learned never to restrict the places one looks for intrigue." He paused, and Faith felt his eyes rake over her from head to sandaled foot.

"Quite so," she heard herself reply. "Why, the people in this room have hatched more diabolical plots than all the terrorists in the world put together. In fact, I'd be surprised if right at this moment someone in this room isn't thinking about murder."

"I'm sure," Justin said smoothly, "but if thoughts could kill I'd've been dead long ago. You don't frighten me, Miss Duvall."

"Does anything?" She met his eyes and held them for a long second. Something about the man provoked her, made her want to challenge him, even though she knew she was playing with fire.

"Low ratings," Ken said hastily. "That's his bogeyman, same as low sales are ours, right? Speaking of sales, Nick, I hope you've had a chance to pick up a copy of my book. If not, I've a large stock of autographed copies—"

It was the most transparent change of subject, but Nick grinned and played along. "No sale," he said. "I read *Come Hell or High Water* as soon as it hit the stands, and I've read *Blood Poisoning,* too," he added, much to Faith's surprise. "I hope I won't embarrass you if I say your awards are richly deserved."

"Embarrass away," Ken said. "We'll live."

"You astonish me," Faith said. "I didn't think you read anything but the Congressional Record and gangsters' memoirs."

"Oh, I love mysteries." There was open provocation in Nick's tone. "Although I generally find the best ones aren't in books. Wouldn't you agree, Miss Duvall?"

Faith gulped, and Ken muttered something about that being the secret of Nick's success. "You see all your stories as mysteries, and you the fearless and brilliant detective, off to track down the villains."

"Funny," Faith remarked, "but I'd never describe Mr. Justin that way."

"And just how would you describe me?" Nick demanded.

"More like a one-man army," Faith said frankly. "In fact, I'd say you had a lot in common with a Sherman tank."

"I'll take that as a compliment."

"I'm sure you would." Faith knew she was being reckless, that she was playing out of her league and that she should say as little as possible. But there was something about the man that, while it daunted her, also drew forth an irresistible desire to respond. To show him that he couldn't bully her.

"Ah, yes," Ken said brightly, determined to play the

role of peacemaker. "Justin the warrior. Very good, Fanny. That will play nicely."

"You make it sound as if image is all that matters," Nick objected.

"Isn't it?" Faith asked. "Isn't your image a large part of your success?"

"And what about your image?" Nick countered. "The woman of mystery, with the shadowy present and the secret past—"

"Now just a minute—" Faith interrupted.

"Do you deny that you refused to allow your publisher to print your photograph on your book jacket?"

"No, but—"

"Why?" Nick pressed his advantage. "It can't be vanity, not with your looks. Shyness? Yet you're no recluse, you're here tonight, accepting an award. Why all the secrecy, Miss Duvall?"

Faith stammered and could not come up with an answer.

"Really, Justin," Ken began, but Nick cut him off.

"You're quite a paradox, Fanny. A face like a Raphael Madonna and a book full of violent death. . . ."

"Violence is a fact of life," Faith said, rather primly. "Everyone's life."

"Yours?" He looked skeptical. "I'd figure you more for church socials and unrequited love."

Faith thought of her father, blown to bits by a bomb in Mississippi, his killers never found. She grew violently, gloriously angry. "You show your prejudices, Mr. Justin. If a man had written *Blood Poisoning,* you'd be gushing about his savage realism and his courage. But because a woman wrote it, you're shocked. Is that fair? Murder can enter anyone's life any time—even my life. Should I be prohibited from dealing with that reality in my work, simply because of my sex?"

Her attack did not deter him for a moment. "Then you plan to continue to write about violence?"

"Yes, I do." And just try to stop me, buster, her tone added. "Why not?"

"Why, indeed?" The smoothness was back in Nick's voice, putting Faith on her guard. "Yet you must see the paradox. Your publisher told me repeatedly that you'd never consent to be interviewed. Yet here you are, vehemently defending your work on camera. Why?"

Faith met his eyes defiantly. "Temptation, Mr. Justin. Sheer temptation."

"How do I tempt you?" He leaned forward.

"When one meets a mind full of prejudices, the temptation to enlighten becomes irresistible." Faith saw the remark hit home, then she turned with a flicker of triumph and took Ken's arm. "I thought you wanted to dance?"

"Oh, by all means, darling," Ken said. "Does that mean I'm irresistible, too?"

Faith, still in shock from her own audacity, didn't reply.

"Don't be so nervous—the war's over," Ken whispered in Faith's ear a moment later, as they danced. "He won't tangle with you again. We'll just dance a bit and then you can disappear. Poof! Fanny Duvall vanishes, leaving Nick Justin with only her glass slipper in his hand."

Faith, acutely conscious of Justin's eyes boring into her back, said nothing. Ken grinned down at her.

"You know, you're beautiful when you're angry."

"You could have told me that you knew him," Faith muttered. "I didn't know we were likely to be targets."

"I don't, really. We met once or twice at parties in London. Seemed a nice enough chap."

"If you like the aggressive type."

"And you don't?"

"I could throw him to the lions and not bat an eyelash."

"I noticed." Ken laughed. "Quite an evening for irony, isn't it? Hear what the band is playing?"

Some enchanted evening, you may see a stranger . . . the sweet lyric made Faith grimace. "I doubt Nick Justin is what Oscar Hammerstein had in mind," she confided. "That is not the look of love."

"One never knows," Ken said. "He can't seem to take his eyes off you. I'd say you've made a conquest."

"When a dog chases a rabbit, has the rabbit made a conquest?"

"Still think he's after your hide?" Ken frowned. "You may be right. I doubt he relishes being one-upped on his own show, especially by a—er, you." Ken pulled her closer. "We'd better give him a good act."

"Act? What do you mean?"

"Misdirection. Justin knows you're hiding something, so make him think being seen with a married man is what gives you that oh-so-obvious guilty conscience."

"You needn't enjoy yourself so much," Faith complained as he cradled her against him. But she saw the sense of his advice, and Ken's friendship comforted her. So she pressed flirtatiously close to him in the dance, and when the song ended she clung to his arm as they went back to the table. She picked up her evening bag.

"You'd better go while the going's good," Ken said. "Act casual, like you're going to powder your nose."

Faith hesitated, trying to find words to thank him for his help. "I'd've never made it through tonight without you."

Ken brushed away her stammering with a careless hand. "When the day comes I can't bail out a lady in distress—"

"I shall never forget you for it," Faith promised.

"That sounds uncommonly like an epitaph," Ken

commented, and grinned. "*Au revoir,* Fanny, and for God's sake look casual."

Nick Justin never budged when Faith ventured to the door. She ran down the hall to the powder room and dashed inside to a stall and closed the door. Alone at last, Faith tried to marshal her thoughts, but found it impossible. She was so nervous her mind buzzed, and she found that conversations carried disastrously well in the tiled bathroom.

"*Newsview!* Can you imagine? I'd've invested in a new dress if I knew Nick Justin would be here. . . ."

Faith sighed. Even here there was no escaping him.

"I actually shook his hand." Another voice. "He's ever so much handsomer in person. Not so angry-looking."

That's what you think, Faith thought.

"And young! Why, he can't be a day over thirty-five!"

"Too young for us, Cheryl," said her companion. "And anyway, he looks dangerous to me. I'm not sure I'd want to tangle with him."

"I would," Cheryl said, and elaborated. Faith put her hands over her ears and tried to block out the conversation.

"Don't waste your time, honey. It's not you or me he's after, it's that blonde. Fanny what's-her-name."

Faith shrank back in the stall, lifting the skirt of her telltale blue dress lest it reveal her identity.

"Oh, her. Well, he always went for artistic types. Married a painter, didn't he?"

"A sculptor, dear, a sculptor. I should know. I have a Cynthia Justin in my office, and that piece cost me plenty."

"Well, I call it unfair. Here we are, both unattached, and he chases a girl who's already got Ken Powell on a string. Some people have all the luck."

The door whooshed shut, and Faith let out a long breath. Cold terror crept through her veins. She wasn't paranoid. Nick Justin was paying an uncommon amount of attention to her, and not for the reason the chatty ladies suspected. He knew she was hiding something; her jibes at him on camera would only whet his appetite to learn the particulars.

And if he did. . . .

She had to leave. Now. Then Justin could search all he liked, but he would never find Fanny Duvall because Fanny Duvall would never be so stupid as to appear anywhere again. If she could just get home safely. . . .

Faith dumped the contents of her small beaded bag onto her lap, frantically searching for some help out of her predicament. All she had in the way of assets were a dime, a subway token and two ten-dollar bills.

The subway was close but the hour was late and she was conspicuously dressed. A cab, then. She'd have to hope to catch one before Nick Justin noticed her absence and began the hunt, but she had enough money to see her safely home.

If only the coast were clear. . . .

Faith waited for some pleasant matrons to leave and sauntered out behind them, using their ample proportions to shield her from view. When Faith reached the elevators a car was waiting; she blessed her luck and darted inside. Perhaps she could make a clean break.

When she reached the ground floor she flew through the lobby and dashed out to the street.

"Cab, miss?"

"Yes, please. Right away." Faith was breathless. Her eyes struggled to adjust to the midnight blackness while she cast anxious glances in all directions. If only she had her glasses. . . .

With a flourish, the doorman flagged a cab and opened the door for her. Faith stumbled over the curb and landed inside the cab. She twisted sideways to guide her trailing skirt carefully past the door frame.

"Thanks so much. You saved my life." She smiled up at the doorman as he shut the door. The cab swung out into traffic.

Faith sank back against the musty cushions and closed her eyes. Safe at last. Then, above her ragged breathing, Faith became aware of another sound, not of her making. Her eyes flew open.

"Hello, Cinderella. It's pumpkin time," said Nick Justin.

Faith screamed.

2

Surprised?" Nick Justin asked, his rich baritone full of amusement.

Faith sputtered a one-word answer. She lunged for the door. Nick intercepted her wrist and forced her backwards. She struggled with him, more from pride than from any hope of escape.

"Stop!" she yelled to the driver as the cab took off like a shot down Fifth Avenue. He ignored her.

Without relaxing his grip on her wrist, Nick pushed her back against the seat, then leaned forward and rapped on the plastic barrier that separated the back and front seats. The door slid open a crack.

"Everything okay, Mr. Justin?"

"Just fine," he said, muffling Faith's protesting mouth against his jacket.

"Where do I take you?"

"Nowhere in particular," Nick said. He winked at the driver. "Why don't you show us New York by night?"

"Yessir. Gotcha." The plastic was pushed shut. Faith's hopes evaporated. She would never make an ally of the cab driver now; Nick had gotten to him first. He'd probably said Faith was a spy, or an embezzler or a congressman's mistress. The cabbie was delirious at the prospect of helping Nick Justin get a hot story.

Faith's depression grew as she realized how complete Nick's preparations were. Her own plans, by comparison, looked more foolhardy by the minute. If she hadn't been in such a panic that she jumped into the cab without looking; if she'd worn her glasses; if she'd had the sense to stay home, as her instincts had warned her all along. . . .

Still, Faith thought as she angrily rallied to her own defense, she wasn't *that* inept. Her plans would have sufficed against any adversary but Nick Justin. His presence had jumped the contest into another league, one where Faith would have to run flat-out to keep one step ahead.

"When you left in such a hurry," Nick said, grinning, "I thought you might have planned a getaway. The least I could do was give you a hand."

"You'll understand if I don't thank you," Faith snapped. He still had her wrist in his grip. She pulled her hand free and glared at him in defiance.

"Feisty," he said appreciatively, with a flash of green in his deep hazel eyes.

"You can't get away with this," Faith muttered, with more confidence than she felt.

"Try me." Nick stretched his long legs into Faith's side of the cab, and flung a careless arm across the back of the seat. Faith flinched, and he chuckled at her instinctive withdrawal.

"You're insufferable," Faith said. Nick's self-satisfied expression made Faith want to punch him. So he had her all figured out, did he?

"Isn't it about time for you to tell me that you'll be missed?" he drawled.

Faith's mind wasn't on his words; she was too conscious of his closeness. It made her claustrophobic. His chest and shoulders blocked her every way she looked, until she felt as if she were strangling. She reached for the door.

He prevented her, his hands rough. "Are you crazy?" he demanded. "You can't jump out of a cab doing fifty."

"I was going to roll down the window. I need the air."

"Oh." Faith realized that she had embarrassed him. Nick reached across to roll down her window, and then rolled down his own. "Better?"

"Some." She wouldn't say thank you.

"Feeling dizzy?" The amusement in his voice infuriated Faith. She felt like a trapped animal, and he knew very well why. She twisted around to stare out the back window. "What are you after now?"

"I'm looking for the cameras. I doubt you'd go to all the trouble to kidnap me and not preserve the results for posterity."

He laughed. "No cameras. There's a tape recorder on the floor."

Faith squinted and could see the edge of the machine; she couldn't reach it without leaning across Nick, an idea she quickly vetoed. She'd just have to settle for making the conversation as unpleasant as possible. If Nick came out badly, he wouldn't use the tape.

Faith readjusted her long skirt, and edged as far from him as possible. She tucked her hands into her lap and composed herself, determined to volunteer no further information.

"Good girl," he said. "Now shall we get on with it?"

"With what?" Faith yelped, alarmed.

"Relax," he said dryly. "I'm not after your body. Your mind is what I want to ravish."

"You've an odd way of showing it."

"First I had to get your attention."

"Next time try an ad in the *New York Times*."

"I prefer my way," he said complacently.

"Of course," Faith snapped. "Why bother to play fair?"

"There's no need to be nasty."

"Oh yes there is, Mr. Justin. When I've been abducted I feel an overwhelming urge to be nasty."

"Nasty enough to call the cops?"

He was testing her. Faith knew she was perfectly within her rights to file charges against him, but Nick Justin's name would attract a lot of publicity. And the first thing she'd have to tell the police would be her real name and her address.

Checkmate. Faith chewed on her lower lip and said nothing.

"That's what I thought," Nick said. "So indulge me for a moment."

"You've gone to a lot of useless trouble for a little conversation."

"Ah, not useless, not with you," he said, and grinned. "I'm sure there will be rewards."

"Go to hell," Faith said. She turned away and watched the spire of the Empire State Building whiz by her window. She could feel Nick's eyes on her, intent in the darkness; they disturbed her in a way not fully accounted for by her predicament.

"Tell me, Mr. Justin." She summoned her best Katharine Hepburn manner to cloak her nervousness. "Do you often resort to abduction?"

"As a matter of fact, you're the first." The note of amusement remained; her grande dame act hadn't fooled him for a moment. "You should be honored."

"As Lincoln said about the man who was tarred and

feathered," Faith said, "if it weren't for the distinction, I'd just as soon walk."

Nick threw back his head and roared, a rich hearty laugh that astounded Faith. His chestnut hair fell down over his forehead, and laugh lines crinkled around his eyes and mouth, giving a boyish cast to his strong features.

Why, he's like another person when he laughs, Faith thought unexpectedly. And then—he needs someone to make him laugh more often.

"So you find me Lincolnesque."

"Hardly." Faith's momentary softness faded and her fury returned. Drat the man—his mind was so quick he could turn anything she said to his advantage.

"They do call me Honest Nick."

"They call you a lot of other things, too."

"The Chinese say you can judge a man's worth by his enemies." He paused. "I'm flattered when corrupt people in high places hate my guts."

"Also innocent people in taxicabs," Faith retorted.

"Quit looking for sympathy. This is costing me a fortune."

"So stop and I'll get out."

"In this neighborhood, at this time of night? Dressed like that? You're taking your life in your hands."

"It beats the pleasure of your company hands down." Faith was pleased to see her remark got under his skin.

"You brought this on yourself," he replied impatiently.

"Oh, really? By what? Living?" Faith's contempt was withering.

"You could have answered a civil question or two."

"I don't recall hearing any."

"All right," he shot back. "Try this. Who the hell are you?"

"The height of civility."

"I'll rephrase it. As they used to say on *To Tell the Truth,* what is your real name and what do you really do?"

"Wait." Something about the phrase troubled Faith; there was something that didn't quite fit. "You're wrong."

"Am I?"

Light dawned. Faith cried, "But that's what they used to say to the *impostors!*"

"If the shoe fits—"

Faith felt his relentless intelligent eyes on her, and she began to turn red. "Impostor? Me?"

"Don't give me that innocent virgin look," he snapped. "I stopped falling for that one when I was in diapers." Nick reached out and touched her face; his fingers trailed along the line of her jaw. "Who are you?"

"You know perfectly well," she said, trying to sound cool and contemptuous. "Fanny Duvall."

"Bull," he said.

"You're entitled to your opinion." Faith hoped her panic didn't show. "It won't be your first mistake."

"I've been in this business for years," he said. "I've got built-in sensors that tell me when people have something to hide. And, lady, you've just gone right off the scale."

Faith pulled away. She looked out her window for landmarks to help her get her bearings. She had to get away, but she couldn't engineer an escape unless she knew where she was.

The cab stopped at a traffic light. Nick reached over to cup Faith's chin between his thumb and fingers. He tilted her face up into the light and forced her to meet his eyes. Her heart beat faster. She found herself noticing how full and long his lashes were, how dark next to the tawny amber of his eyes.

And what did he see in her face? Confusion and fear, lost eyes that stared myopically out of a pinched face, a telltale blush.

"There is no Fanny Duvall," Nick Justin said softly. "Is there?"

"Of course not. I'm an illusion."

"Exactly," he said, with a jump in his voice that reminded Faith of a cat pouncing on a mouse.

"And my book, that's an illusion too, I suppose?" Faith's voice sounded high-pitched and tense, even to her.

"The book is real enough," Nick said, "but you're a phony from the word go." He stretched out along the seat and dropped his arm around Faith's shoulders. The shock of his hand against her bare skin made her jump.

"I'm a good listener, Fanny," he said. His voice was surprisingly gentle. "Why don't you tell me the whole story?"

With his hand on her shoulder he could feel her body tremble. Faith had never felt so vulnerable. His maleness assaulted her: his thigh pressing against hers, his musky scent filling her nostrils. His caressing voice was seductive enough to make her forget that a tape recorder spun at her feet, that he was on a job, that all he really cared about was her story. Faith bit her lip and steeled herself against the desire to yield.

"Why don't you just drop me off at a subway?" she asked coldly. "You're wasting your valuable time."

"Not at all. I'm enjoying this."

He was—Faith could see it in his eyes. A childhood memory rose: Sherlock Holmes crying, "Come, Watson! The game is a-foot!" with just such relish as Nick Justin betrayed now. And she was the game.

Faith felt a rush of anger. "You must be hard-up for female companionship. Though that doesn't surprise me, considering how you get your kicks."

"Attacking me won't work," Nick said calmly. "When I'm on a story nothing deters me. I've got a one-track mind."

"Just a nose for news, is that it? A regular bloodhound. I'm amazed you find me so stimulating."

"You underrate yourself," Nick said. "Consider the facts. A woman writes a novel. She's so anxious to protect her identity that she writes under an assumed name, handles all her negotiations by mail. No one at Caldwell Publishing has ever laid eyes on Fanny Duvall.

"Now comes the weird part. The book gets nominated for an Edgar. Given Fanny Duvall's character, you'd think wild horses couldn't drag her to an awards dinner. So I go, fully expecting the lady won't be present—and what do I find?"

A consummate fool, Faith thought.

"Lo and behold, who trots up to receive her award, but a Miss Fanny Duvall. Do you wonder I've got some questions to ask that lady?"

"Like what?" The words slipped out against Faith's better judgment.

"For now, I'm toying with two possibilities."

"Which are?"

"A: the woman is Fanny Duvall, for unknown reasons breaking with her past behavior. Or, B: the woman is not Fanny Duvall, but an impersonator. I think you'd agree it has to be one or the other."

"You haven't lost me yet," Faith said.

"So, let's say you're not Fanny Duvall."

Faith sighed. "How did I know you'd pick that one first?"

"If you're pretending to be her, you must have inside knowledge of her habits, because you couldn't risk being the second Fanny Duvall to arrive."

His hand slid down along her arm. "Maybe the publisher asked you to double for her. Pictures of you would be good publicity—"

"But if I'm a stand-in," Faith protested, "I wouldn't know anything about the real Fanny Duvall. I'd only know what the publisher told me to say. So I couldn't help you at all."

"That's why I'm not fond of that solution," he said. "It doesn't ring my bells."

"Can't have that," Faith said lightly.

"If you came on your own," Nick went on, "that's much better. You could always be a nut who thinks she's Fanny Duvall the way some people, I'm told, think they're Napoleon." He paused to inspect her critically. "But for the moment I'm prepared to rule that out."

"Thanks so much," Faith drawled.

"Or you could be someone who knew the real author wouldn't be there. Which means you know who the real author is. And if you've got a pipeline to Fanny Duvall, then I'm home-free."

"If she's a hermit, she wouldn't be likely to sit down to a cozy tea with Nick Justin, would she?"

"No, but a cozy tea with you might do just as well. You can fill me in on all the gory details."

"What if there aren't any gory details? Honestly, I doubt this story is up to your standards. No spies or kickbacks or international drug rings, so why bother?"

"Because I've been challenged," he replied levelly. "She's drawn a cloak around herself and dared me to pull it off. So I will. She's asked for it."

"You have a twisted mind, Mr. Justin. How you get from point A to point B defies logic."

"Ah, point A," Nick said. "Back to point A. Remember? That you are, yourself, the mysterious Fanny Duvall."

"But you said you don't believe that."

He gave her a long appraising look as he replied. "Not much, no."

"Why not? I don't look like your idea of a writer? All blondes are empty-headed and can't count past ten, let alone write?"

Nick grinned. "You're determined that I underestimate you, aren't you?"

"I—of course not."

"You're a smart girl, Fanny. Would you go to such trouble to publish in secrecy and then blow it all for one moment of glory?" He looked at her in cool appraisal, as if she were a painting he might buy. "Of course, you could be colossally vain. Or—better—the circumstances that compelled you to secrecy could have changed."

"What circumstances?" Faith asked hollowly.

"Say you had a husband who didn't want you to write, and the husband's no longer around. Or maybe you're reckless enough to believe you could elude any media coverage—"

"She might be just plain dumb," Faith said in a small voice.

"No way. The woman who wrote *Blood Poisoning* has a first-class mind."

"She could have miscalculated," Faith persisted. "Thought the awards would be informal, like a club meeting. That no press would be there."

"Wrong," Nick said. "You see, she *wanted* to be found out."

"What?" Faith jumped away from the seat in shock.

"She wanted to be found out," Nick repeated.

"That's preposterous."

"No, it isn't. Ask any psychologist."

"I will not," Faith said angrily. "It's utter nonsense."

"Haven't you heard of killers who send notes that say 'Stop me before I kill again'? Whatever sort of double life Fanny Duvall has been leading, I think the pressures have grown to be too much for her to handle. She wants her secret out in the open. Consciously or unconsciously, she's begging to be unmasked."

"That's ridiculous," Faith said, but her confidence was ebbing. As if he sensed her lack of conviction, Nick reached out and took Faith by the shoulders and turned her to face him. His fingers lingered on the pulse beating in her neck.

"So you see," he said, "I'm doing you a favor."

"Out of the goodness of your heart, no doubt." Faith spoke sharply, annoyed with herself at having betrayed weakness to him. "You won't get a thing out of this."

"Probably not," Nick said, angered. "Do you have any idea how many stories I kill out of common decency? Or how many details wind up on the cutting room floor because I don't deal in sensationalism?"

"Oh, you're a saint," Faith said. Her voice turned ice cold. "You expect me to believe you wouldn't use whatever you could get on Fanny Duvall? She's probably the only chance you have to put some punch into this story on the MWA, so don't give me that line that you want to satisfy your curiosity for its own sake. I know the difference between a good story and no story at all."

"Oh, you do, do you? Maybe you're a writer after all."

Faith's blood chilled. She had made another mistake.

"Maybe you can explain this to me," Nick continued, in a menacingly quiet tone. "Here's the real kicker. Why in hell, after jeopardizing her security to receive an award that's supposed to mean so much to her, does the damn woman leave without even taking her prize?"

He reached down to the floor and tossed aside a newspaper near his feet. Faith gasped. A ceramic bust looked up at her, as damning a bit of evidence as any baby abandoned on church steps. Her Edgar.

And if that's not proof I'm not the real Fanny Duvall, I don't know what is, Faith thought.

"I know it's supposed to be a glass slipper I try on for size," Nick drawled, "but I have to play the cards you dealt me. This is your Edgar, isn't it?"

"Where did you get that?"

"Where do you think?"

Mentally Faith retraced her steps: when she'd fled the ballroom, her Edgar had been sitting on the table next to Ken Powell's. Nick must have walked right up and taken it.

So he had never believed her ruse; he had guessed her plans right from the start.

"What, no comment?" he prodded. "No 'get your filthy hands off my Edgar'?"

"Possession is nine-tenths of the law," Faith snapped back, "so maybe *you're* Fanny Duvall."

Nick roared with laughter. "Two points to the blonde," he said. "Okay, feisty, if you want me to keep it, I'll keep it."

Faith could imagine the inquisition she'd undergo if she tried to reclaim her prize, and she wasn't sure she could stand up under a fusillade of Nick Justin's questions. Besides, at the moment, she didn't particularly want her Edgar back. Not when every time she looked at it she'd remember how foolish she'd been.

"Keep it and put it where the sun doesn't shine," she muttered.

"Such language."

"Have I been sufficiently humiliated for one night? You've proven I'm not Fanny Duvall, so can I go now?"

Faith looked out the window and was shocked to see the lights of Manhattan streaming away on her left. They must have crossed over to Brooklyn and she hadn't even noticed. If Nick took her seriously and let her out here, how would she get home? Hitchhike?

Nick's voice pierced her thoughts. "I haven't said you're not Fanny Duvall," he remarked, as if posing a casual question about the weather.

"I left my Edgar behind. That's proof enough."

"Hold on. You left your Edgar with Ken Powell to take home for you. That's hardly abandonment."

"What do you mean?" Faith was genuinely puzzled.

"Come off it, Fanny." Nick's voice grated. "You and Ken Powell are having an affair. That's obvious. I guess the fact that he's married and has kids means nothing to you. Well, hell, you might have a husband stashed somewhere yourself, who knows?"

Faith laughed bitterly. "That's ridiculous."

"You deny Powell's your lover?"

"My lover?" Faith was aghast. "How could you think so?" Belatedly, she remembered she'd worked hard to give him that impression, and she blushed in embarrassment.

"Because it fits," Nick argued. "Then all the pieces of the puzzle go together. And you have a classic motive to go to the banquet: you wanted to expose your affair."

"Oh, my God."

"I know Alicia Powell," Nick went on grimly. "She's the old-fashioned type. If she found out her husband cheated on her, she'd have him in the divorce courts quick enough. And then you'd have Ken all to yourself."

"Then why did I run away from you?" Faith demanded. "Why didn't I walk up to you and say 'Please put us on TV so Ken's wife will see us together and blow her stack'?"

"Because Powell saw through your little scheme. He told you if you weren't discreet you'd lose him. I saw you two quarreling in the hall before dinner."

Just her luck. It would do no good to protest that the "quarrel" Nick thought he'd seen had been Ken pleading with her to stay.

"Damn it, Fanny." Nick looked as if he wanted to shake the stuffing out of her. "Can't you see he's using you?"

"He's using me!" Faith cried in astonishment. "That's rich, coming from you. Ken never kidnaped me!"

"No, he didn't have to, did he? You were only too willing—"

"Stop! I won't listen to this," Faith said, furiously defending her friend. "Ken Powell is a gentleman. He cares about what happens to me. Not like you. All you care about is your precious story—not the poor person whose life you kick to bits. Ken would never hurt me or exploit me. He's gentle and kind and caring."

"And married. Or have you conveniently forgotten that?" Nick shouted. "But what does a little detail like that matter? All that warmth must make him terrific in bed."

"That's more than anyone could say for you," Faith shot back. "You're so cold and self-centered and manipulative that you don't respond to anything but facts and figures. Your feelings are dead at the roots."

Something snapped in the rigid control in Nick's face. "Like hell they are," he muttered. Before Faith could brace herself to resist, his arms came around her, pulling her against him, and his mouth came down ruthlessly against hers.

Faith nearly screamed from shock. And the shock didn't fade as the kiss went on—if anything, it grew worse. What was he doing to her? Her head whirled with confused emotions as the blood pounded deafeningly in her ears.

I'm frightened, Faith told herself firmly. That's why my heart is pounding. And I'm angry. I hate Nick Justin, hate everything about him.

Of course she did. And yet—

Yet she had trouble holding on to her anger. Couldn't force herself to fight against him. As Nick's arms tightened possessively hers grew limper, and the tight line of her lips softened against the pressure of his.

Nick made a small, satisfied sound and deepened the kiss, his tongue probing the sweetness of her mouth. His hands began to trace marvelous patterns through Faith's long silky hair, to skate dangerously across the soft exposed flesh of her back. Faith felt her resistance ebb away, to be replaced by sensations she'd never felt before—intolerable heat, and a driving pulse that blocked out all the other sounds in the universe. Her body began to stir against him, responding of its own accord, oblivious to the startled messages of her brain.

What was happening to her? The Faith Daniels who sang so sweetly in the church choir should be appalled to be kissed so intimately by a stranger, she told herself. Appalled!

But she wasn't. When Nick pulled her closer Faith hadn't the smallest desire to pound her fists against his back or kick his shins. Even though this man was her most dangerous enemy. Even though he could topple all she'd built in her life that mattered.

Even though she knew Nick kissed her only out of exasperation.

Some far corner of her mind recognized these truths, but they seemed insignificant compared to the tide of pleasure rushing over her. Faith gave herself over to Nick's touch, letting him do whatever he wanted with her helpless body, reveling in the power of his chest and arms. After long moments of temptation, she even found the courage to touch him back. Faith explored with tentative, shaking fingers the roughness of his jaw and the velvet smoothness of his hair, hoping that if she made her touch delicate enough her response might escape his notice entirely. . . .

No such luck. A shock rippled over Nick's body; his breathing caught and then started again, unevenly. Faith's eyes opened in alarm to see him loosening the buttons of his shirt.

"No," she gasped, conscious at last. She didn't know if the word was directed to Nick or to her own traitorous self. It didn't matter; he held her tightly as she tried to move away, forcing her to feel his strength and her vulnerability. The fury had drained out of his face, leaving a taut hunger that frightened her as his anger never could.

"God, you're beautiful." His voice seemed to come from another planet. He bent down to her and Faith, afraid of what would happen if she let him kiss her again, jerked her head away. He kissed her throat instead.

"Please, stop," she begged breathlessly. Nick's lips trailed across her naked shoulder. She moaned with pleasure and felt her shivering response register inside him.

"You're a lousy liar, Fanny," he murmured, and his mouth caught hers with driving force.

This has got to stop, Faith thought desperately. Nick's intensity frightened her, but far worse was a hint of the same intensity stirring within herself. Where did it come from—the ache in her breasts, the burning emptiness in her center that spread like a slow fire through her body? Faith knew a sudden reckless, dangerous longing to make love to Nick Justin, here and now, and was astonished by the force of her feelings. She had never wanted a man so much—never thought she could.

A picture flashed into her mind: Nick, naked, intense, sliding the dress from her shoulders. . . .

No. Faith's mind recoiled from her thoughts in horror. It wasn't as if Nick were attracted to her as a person; quite the opposite. Nothing was more plain than his contempt for Fanny Duvall. He was playing with Faith, hoping to lower her defenses and make her confide in him. And she was falling for it.

Damn her inexperience; it left her so vulnerable, so open to deception. Her fiancé had been the only lover in her life, and Harald, for all his devastating looks and undeniable experience, had never made her feel anything like this. Faith felt tears of humiliation form under her closed eyelids. How could she want a man who was only using her?

Nick let go of her abruptly and sat up, brushing his hair out of his eyes with long, tense fingers. He said nothing, and his taut, shuttered face gave no clue to his feelings. Faith stared at him in bewilderment. Had she bored him so quickly?

"Here." He pushed a handkerchief into her hand. Faith reached her fingers up to her cheeks and realized she was crying.

"Oh." Faith felt mortified and childish. She held the linen up to her face longer than necessary, hoping to compose herself. Nick watched her from his corner of the cab, his face unreadable, a vein pounding in his temple.

Sweet Lord, he's attractive, Faith thought suddenly. She studied his profile with hungry eyes: the eyelashes a dark slash against his cheekbone, the compressed, sensual line of his mouth. Faith remembered, vividly, the feeling of that mouth against her skin, and her insides twisted in pain. What had happened to the clinical detachment she'd always felt when she looked at a man's body? Five minutes in his arms had changed her forever.

"For God's sake, Fanny." He spoke as he would to a child. "This is not the end of the world."

The note of amusement in his voice sparked her into anger. "Go to hell," Faith said, and meant it. "And leave me alone."

"Why should I?"

"Oh, I forgot." Faith's voice stung like a whip. "Mr. Justin doesn't live in the same universe as we mere mortals. He doesn't have any rules.

"But I've got news for you. I don't care how many rackets you've busted or criminals you've put in jail. That doesn't give you a license to terrorize anyone who crosses your path. There are still a few innocent people left in this world, you know, even if you're so jaded and cynical you wouldn't know an innocent if you tripped over him. You're so used to invading people's privacy you've forgotten their rights exist. You might as well be the Gestapo."

Nick said nothing, but Faith thought she saw a softening in the harsh planes of his face. She waited for a moment, hoping for some words to make a truce between them. But no words came.

Uncomfortably, she turned to stare out of the window. For the first time in ages, the streets looked familiar. Her heartbeat quickened as she recognized the neighborhood.

"You may not believe this," Nick began at last.

"Try me," Faith said absently, her mind riveted on the boutiques and restaurants of Columbus Avenue. She knew exactly where she was: she was practically in her own backyard. Now she could plan her escape.

"Look," Nick said abruptly, "I've lost track of the number of stories that I've killed because their news value wasn't worth the destruction they'd bring to people's personal lives. Give me some credit. I know the difference between a crook who's defrauding the public and needs to be called to account, and someone who's made a mistake and regrets it."

"So you set yourself up as judge and jury," Faith taunted. "You decide who's to be forgiven and who's to be punished?"

"Damn it, it's not that way at all!" Nick exploded.

"Well, I've already had my punishment, judge, so why not just stop the cab and let me go?"

Nervously, Faith watched the blocks pass. She was within yards of her own apartment now, yet dared not make a run for it and risk leading Nick straight to her home and her real identity.

But she knew every subway stop in the area. If she

could make it to a subway, she could lead him away on a false trail, then double back to her apartment. If she could get a head start, take him by surprise—

Nick was speaking quietly, his hand on her arm. "Listen. I know you're in trouble. I can protect you, if you'll just trust me. I'm not out to get you, Fanny."

She forced her gaze away from the window, lest she telegraph her intentions. "Oh, really?" she asked coldly. "You could've fooled me."

"What are you so scared of?"

"You!" she cried involuntarily. "Isn't it obvious?"

"Why?"

There was no answer for that, none she could risk giving. She glared across at Nick and was surprised to read concern in his eyes, tiny lines around his mouth and brow that might almost be worry.

"I don't understand you, Fanny," Nick said slowly. Faith could tell they were words he seldom said. Under any other circumstances she would have been flattered by that admission, at having reached a chink in his armor. Just now, she could think only of her escape.

"Darn right you don't understand," she muttered.

"Then tell me about it. I'll help you, if I can."

Nick had her hand between both of his. Faith felt that dreadful melting in her stomach again. If only she could trust him! For a moment, she longed to throw her arms around his neck and tell him everything that had happened to her from the day she was born.

Faith steeled herself against the traitorous impulse. It's only a trick, she reminded herself sternly. Just another page from his book of tactics . . . the soft voice, the sympathetic eyes.

"Oh, you're good, Mr. Justin. You're wasting your time in journalism—you should go on the stage." She put as much contempt as possible into her tone, afraid he had seen her moment of near-surrender. "But I have nothing else to say to you. I've played the fool enough for one night.''

She turned away and stared resolutely out of the window.

Nick cursed: a short, sharp oath that stunned her with its violence. Faith felt a tremor run through her body. She knew all too well the effects of frustrating Nick Justin.

Dead ahead, Columbus Circle loomed. Its honeycomb of subways beckoned to Faith. Several train lines crossed here; if she could get a head start she might lose Nick entirely in the maze of trains and make a clean getaway.

Faith's heart began to race. If they could just catch a red light at this intersection! She stole a glance at the electronic meter, clicking away, its total staggering. Nick would have to pay the cabbie—that would hold him up for a few precious seconds. And meanwhile she'd hitch up her skirt and run down into the dark tunnels. . . .

She tensed her body to spring for the locked door. The Coliseum rose on her right, the south end of Central Park rolled away on her left. This is it, Faith thought, now or never. She held her breath.

The light turned red.

Before the cab's wheels stopped turning she'd slipped the catch on the door and was off. She ran, dodging the few cabs still on the street, making a beeline for the subway entrance.

Faith heard her name explode into the night air. Nick Justin called after her and cursed. She didn't look back. Blood drummed in her ears; she lifted her slim skirt high about her knees and pushed on, ignoring the pain in her feet from the sleek Italian sandals that were never meant for running.

The slam of the cab door rang through the night. So much for her head start—thirty, forty seconds. No more. Faith's fingers dug into her purse and fastened on her subway token. The cavernous entrance with its scores of stairs yawned ominously before her.

For a moment she wanted to give up rather than enter that dungeon alone. But that was something Faith Daniels would do—and tonight, for better or worse, she was Fanny Duvall.

Faith lifted her skirt higher and ran down the stairs into the subway.

3

~~~~~~~~~~~~

Faith raced down the stairs. Twice she nearly lost control of her footing, yet she pushed herself. Faster. Faster.

"Fanny?"

Nick's voice, resonant with anger, echoed down the stairwells and passageways. She heard his feet pound as he ran down the stairs.

Faith shoved a token into the slot and slammed through the barrier. By day, she knew this station like the back of her hand; by night, she might be entering the Twilight Zone. The slightest sound was magnified tenfold, so that the slap, slap of her sandals on the concrete floor sounded like cannon.

Faith fought for breath. Her chest hurt, as if a fist had closed around her heart and kneaded it as if it were bread dough.

"Fanny!" The echoes again. "Damn it! Wait!"

He's getting closer, Faith thought. She must get on a train and leave the station before Nick could catch up with her. She needed luck, and so far this night luck had not been with her.

Faith glanced at her watch: one o'clock. Trains ran infrequently at this hour; she could be stranded fifteen minutes or more on the platform.

Well, I have to try, she thought grimly. She cast a glance at the IRT platform. Empty, and no sounds that would indicate an approaching train. And only one train stopped on this platform, the #1 local.

Faith turned away and ran down the stairs to the IND platform. At least with the IND, she had better odds. Several trains stopped there. Maybe she'd catch one as it pulled in.

A stab of pain ran up her left leg. Faith leaned against a pillar and tugged off her sandals. Drat these shoes—elegant, but not practical. She caught the shoes by their straps, hiked up her skirt with her free hand, and kept running.

Faith's mind spun with escape plans. Should she try for a train that would take her home? Then if Nick followed her, she would lead him straight to her true identity.

What, then?

Perhaps she should take a train headed away from home, but get off at the first stop, run up to the street and hope to find a cab. Even if Nick managed to get on the train, he might not catch up to her by the first stop—

"Fanny? Are you crazy?"

Faith tried to guess Nick's location by the echo of his voice. It sounded like he had tried the IRT platform first. He would soon see that she wasn't there, and would head downstairs to the IND.

Faith leaned over the edge of the closest track and looked down into the tunnel. She strained her eyes. Did she see lights approaching, or were they a figment of her hopeful imagination?

"Fanny! Wait!"

That voice was not her imagination. She looked over her shoulder. Nick Justin bounded down the stairs, three at a time.

"Damn it, Fanny! When I get hold of you—"

Faith ran down the platform, wishing it were infinite, wondering what would happen when Nick inevitably caught her.

A train chugged into the station and stopped halfway down the platform. Faith breathed a prayer of thanksgiving and darted inside the car opposite her, happy to see the doors whoosh shut almost immediately.

She had been lucky: the train was several cars shorter than it would be during a rush hour. She was fairly certain that, with the distance Nick had to travel, there was no way he could have boarded the train before the doors closed.

So she was safe after all.

Maybe.

Faith caught her breath and glanced dubiously at her surroundings. The subway car was illumined only by the faint emergency lights, and the car's only occupant was stretched out full-length across several seats. He glanced up at Faith with a benign smile, looking at her shimmering dress and disheveled hair as if she were some apparition from a dream.

For the first time Faith realized how odd she must appear—a woman in flight, out of breath, shoes in hand, her pale gown shining in the dim light—

Good heavens, I look like a runaway bride, she thought. All I need is a bouquet.

She could not suppress a bitter laugh as she walked to the end of the car and pushed through the door. Better to be cautious, she thought. Move toward the center of the train, where she might find some fellow travelers, and safety in numbers.

The second car she entered was empty. The third had a half-dozen reasonably alert people, clustered together near the center of the car, each carefully avoiding staring at Faith's unusual attire. For once grateful for New York subway etiquette, Faith turned to settle into her seat when she saw something that froze her breath in her throat.

A flash of black. A sleeve, or a shoulder. Back behind her, in the car she'd just passed through. The car that had been deserted.

Nick Justin was on the train.

Somehow, he had made it on board, perhaps by vaulting over the coupling between cars; now he was searching for Faith. She leapt up and ran for the far door, trying to put distance between herself and her nemesis, though she knew it was futile. Another car or two, and she'd be at the end of the train, and where could she run then? Unless the train pulled into a station before Nick caught up to her. . . .

Lost in her panicked thoughts, Faith did not notice how dark the car was she had entered, or how empty. She didn't even see the shape barreling toward her as she stood silhouetted in the light from the car she had just left, the jeweled brooch on her dress flashing seductively.

She felt a bump that sent her sprawling, knocked her shoes from her hand; she heard the rip of tearing fabric, the crunch of a closing door.

Two seconds' time, no more. Faith had only seen a dark shadow rush by, yet when she reached up to the bodice of her dress, she felt shreds of silk hanging down where it had been ripped. Her brooch—her mother's treasured aquamarine and diamond brooch—was gone.

Faith screamed. In her shock she didn't even realize that she screamed Nick Justin's name. She pulled the door open and staggered barefoot after the thief, not from any hope of catching him—for what would she do if she did?—but simply in hope of seeing him clearly.

Even in the well-lit car, all Faith saw was a blur of blue. Jeans and a navy jacket on a slim male figure about two inches taller than she.

Some description, Faith thought sadly, as she chased down the car to the opposite door. If only he would turn around so she could see his face—

But he didn't. Faith paused in the doorway, resigned to her loss, feeling dangerously close to tears. She scarcely noticed when, off in the shadows, the figure in blue bumped up against a figure in black. Only after they lingered there, curiously immobile, their bodies blocking the aisle, did Faith realize that the men were struggling against each other—the figure in blue trying to break away, the figure in black holding him fast.

And the figure in black was Nick Justin.

"Nick!" she cried, and ran toward the men. "He stole my jewelry!"

"Oh, did he?" There was less force than usual behind Nick's baritone, as if he were short of breath, but he seemed to have remarkably little trouble subduing Faith's assailant, whom she could now see to be a boy of about eighteen.

"You're crazy, lady," sputtered the youth. "I never—"

"What's happening here?" The conductor interrupted in a nervous tone. "Trouble?"

"Call the cops," Nick said shortly. "The lady's been robbed."

"That's bull, mister. I never—"

In one swift impatient move, Nick produced the aquamarine brooch from the side pocket of the boy's Windbreaker.

"I see," said the conductor, relieved that no further

action would be required on his part except to alert the police. "How did it happen?"

Faith told her story in two brief sentences, sank into a seat, and began to shake. Nick handed the boy over to the conductor and came to Faith's side.

"Are you all right?" he asked gently, and Faith nodded, not trusting herself to speak. Nick sat down beside her and put his arm around her trembling shoulders, drawing her close to him.

"You shouldn't have run away," he murmured. Faith, in a fog, leaned her head against his shoulder and closed her eyes. She only knew that she had been frightened and now she was warm and safe and indescribably exhausted.

"I'll take you home," she heard Nick murmur, "as soon as we finish with the police."

"Police?" Faith repeated drowsily, his words not penetrating her fogged mind.

"You'll have to file charges. You don't want that kid on the street."

"Course not," Faith said, but only slowly did she begin to grasp the implications of Nick's words. Her eyes opened.

"Police?" she asked again, but with a note of fear in her voice.

"Don't worry," Nick said, all matter-of-fact reassurance. "I'll stay with you through the interrogation, the lineup, everything. It's not bad. And the trial will be a piece of cake."

"Trial?" she echoed hollowly.

"Don't worry." He grinned. "I make a hell of a witness."

"I'm sure you do," Faith said numbly, but her mind was spinning. Interrogation. Trial. What was she going to do? She could scarcely file charges as Fanny Duvall, could she? She would have to give the police her real name and her address.

Which meant Nick Justin would have them too.

Then the truth would come out. Who Fanny Duvall was . . . and what she had done. Everyone would learn about her book, her subterfuges, her double life. Then would come the wrenching scenes with her aunt Prue and with Harald, the recriminations, the anger—

She couldn't go to the police.

Nick saw the panic in her eyes and misinterpreted the cause. "Don't worry," he said. "I know you were scared, but it's all over now. Nobody's going to hurt you."

His words twisted Faith's heart. *That's what you think,* she thought angrily; *if this story comes out, I'll be hurt beyond repair.* Yet how could she protect herself? Faith feared her only choice was to somehow get away, to leave Nick Justin before he could get her to the police station.

Faith sighed. She was surprised to discover that she would much, much rather not run away again. She looked up into Nick's greenish hazel eyes and the concern she saw there spread a warm glow through her body. Damn it, why was he being such a nice guy? She wouldn't mind running out on the cynical, ruthless Nick Justin, the man who seemed only interested in her story. But to have him act as if he really cared what happened to her, and then to leave him to deal with the police alone—

She could imagine what he would think of her then.

"What's wrong?"

"I don't feel well," she hedged. That was true enough. When she imagined the contempt settling back into Nick's eyes, she felt sick to her stomach.

"Take it easy." He drew her head back against his shoulder and stroked her hair comfortingly. "We'll be in the station soon."

Faith sighed. She might as well enjoy it, this last moment of calm before the storm broke. Any minute now, the train would pull into the station, and they would again become enemies, hunter and prey. She would have to run.

Run. Her shoes were back in the other car. She stirred as if to move and Nick restrained her.

"Where are you going?"

"My shoes—they're in the other car."

"Stay here," he ordered. "I'll go."

Faith had no more than closed her eyes before he was back, her delicate sandals dangling incongruously from his long fingers.

"Here. I didn't see your purse—"

"That's okay. I've got it here. He didn't grab my purse—just pulled off the brooch and ran."

"That's too bad about your brooch," Nick commented. "It looks like an heirloom. It must mean a lot to you."

"It was my mother's." Faith spoke the truth without thinking.

"Was?"

"Yes," Faith said softly. "She's dead."

"Sorry." There was a moment when Faith knew he was about to probe for more information, and she cursed herself for having volunteered any facts about herself. But he only remarked, "I'm afraid it'll be a while before you get the brooch back, you know. Evidence—"

"I know." And if Faith didn't file charges, she would never get Cecily's brooch back. Yet, now, that seemed a small loss compared to the loss of Nick Justin's regard. Faith bit her lip to keep from saying so. Fortunately, Nick couldn't see her face; he had dropped to one knee and was lifting her ankle.

"You see, Cinderella," he said in a strangely moving voice, "I managed to come up with the slipper after all."

His eyes met hers and Faith began to tremble as he slid

the sandal onto her foot. For a moment, the attraction between them was so strong it seemed to have a shape and weight of its own. Faith leaned forward, drawn toward him irresistibly, stunned by what she felt. She thought, I shall dream about that look in his eyes. . . .

The train slowed to a stop. 125th Street. Once the station had meant safety to Faith; now she dreaded having to leave the train.

Nick rose and looked down at her, and Faith hurriedly disciplined her face lest he see too much. He had a suspicious nature to begin with, and if he should guess that she meant to run away again—

Odd, how desolate she felt at the thought of leaving him. And less than an hour ago she was sure she hated Nick Justin.

Faith trailed slowly after him as he marched her assailant off the train into the arms of two waiting policemen. Faith offered her account of what happened in a dazed, flat voice. Then she answered question after question, all the while wondering how on earth she could manage to escape. It seemed an eternity before she finally heard the rumble of an approaching train.

At last the train pulled in on the opposite side of the platform. Going downtown. Back home.

Faith didn't look at the track, didn't give any sign she'd even heard the train. She waited, with quickened breath, until the last possible moment. Then she ran the ten feet across the platform and jumped inside the train just as the doors closed.

"Fanny! What the hell?"

Nick cursed as the train began to move. The last thing Faith saw was Nick Justin as he ran down the platform, his white shirt a blur. He shouted her name.

* * *

"You mean," Bonnie's blue eyes grew round with disbelief, "you could turn around and get on another train? Faith! You have nerves of steel!"

"Nerves of jelly," Faith said dryly. "I was scared to death the whole time. But I had to get away—there was no way I could risk finishing with the police." She poked aimlessly at the lid on a box of chocolate donuts. "I hope Nick's testimony is enough to hold that kid. Maybe he filed an assault charge, or something."

Bonnie eyed Faith shrewdly and poured her a cup of steaming coffee. "Conscience bothering you?"

"You don't know how much," Faith admitted.

"This is a red-letter night. Faith Daniels sins. I'm sure you'll be forgiven just one."

Faith laughed. "More than one, I'm afraid." She looked around the bright dining alcove, with its familiar splashes of yellow and orange. She expected to feel calm and safe now that she was back in her own apartment, but reassurance did not come. She would almost be relieved if burly policemen were to knock on the door and drag her away.

Faith looked at the impromptu breakfast her roommate had prepared, and appreciated, once again, Bonnie Chandler's innate kindness. Somehow Bonnie always sensed when Faith needed to talk. "You're a lifesaver," Faith said.

"That's what roommates are for," Bonnie said complacently.

"And you love getting up in the middle of the night to listen to my raving."

"Hey, if you think you can walk in here looking like something from an Italian movie, and go to bed before you tell me all the details—"

"You've heard them," Faith groaned. "Sheer hell from beginning to end."

Bonnie grinned. "And who was the girl who was always complaining that her life was too dull for words?"

"Tonight wasn't exactly what I had in mind."

"I think it sounds marvelous. Nick Justin and Ken Powell in one evening!"

"It was perfectly horrid," Faith sniffed.

"Everything?"

"Well . . ." She remembered, in a flash, Nick Justin's arms around her.

"I thought so." Bonnie sounded smug. "You're a changed woman, Faith. I could see that the moment you walked in."

"Nonsense." Faith knew she was blushing.

"Huh. You should see your eyes shimmer when you say his name. Justin must be dynamite."

"He's arrogant, insulting and high-handed," Faith said, "and I found him perfectly beastly."

"Of course, he did save your life, sort of," Bonnie observed. Amusement danced in her eyes. "There's that."

"He owed it to me," Faith said defensively. "It was his fault I was on that train in the first place. After all, he abducted me!"

"I don't know as that would stand up in court. You did get into the cab willingly enough—"

"Only because I couldn't see him."

"So now it's Nick's fault you weren't wearing your glasses?"

"Whose side are you on?" Faith demanded.

"Yours, dear." Bonnie took another donut from the box, and gestured to Faith to do the same. "Will you please eat one of these, at least? You're skinny as a rail, you can afford the calories. It's downright disgusting that you don't eat in a crisis."

Faith laughed, and picked up one of the chocolate confections.

"What's Nick Justin like?" Bonnie asked. "Give me a one-word description."

"Just one word?" Faith wrinkled her brow as she nibbled at the donut. "What's that adjective that Archie Goodwin is always using to describe himself? That quality of going on, no matter what."

Bonnie had introduced Faith to Rex Stout's classic detective series, and knew instantly what Faith meant. "Intrepid!" she cried.

"That's it," Faith agreed. "Absolutely intrepid."

"Is he as bright as he sounds on TV?"

"Smart as a steel trap and twice as lethal."

"Handsome?"

Faith deliberated. "No. But compelling. And younger than he looks on TV."

"But not handsome." There was a teasing note in Bonnie's voice. "You're blushing again. I suppose he kissed you?"

Faith nodded. "A bit."

"And?"

Faith couldn't reply. Bonnie took one look at her roommate's crimson cheeks and shining eyes, and sighed. "I knew it. You've gone off the deep end at last. So what are you going to do about Harald?"

"Nothing," Faith said firmly.

"Nothing? You can't mean to go ahead and marry him."

"Why not? For heaven's sake, Bonnie, it's not as if I'll ever see Nick Justin again."

"Don't be so sure," Bonnie warned. "And anyway, you should see now you don't belong with Harald."

"You just don't like Harald," Faith said accusingly.

"No I don't." Bonnie's tone was hard. "He's an opportunist and he can't be trusted. He saw the chance to marry Harrison Daniels' reputation and Cecily Daniels' money, and get an innocent blond wife in the bargain. Face it, Faith, with your looks, your name and your money, you're an ideal politician's wife. And Harald grabbed you."

Faith frowned. "You don't think he loves me?"

"Maybe." Bonnie sighed, unwilling to condemn even a man she disliked. "I couldn't say, and I don't care. I'm saying *you* don't love *him*."

"Yes, I do," Faith insisted stubbornly, but she lacked the conviction she usually brought to this argument.

"But you don't enjoy sleeping with him."

"I enjoy it," Faith said with precision. "I just don't—um —don't get carried away—"

"Then why on earth did you say you'd marry him?" Bonnie asked bluntly. "Why not wait for a man who does—um, carry you away?"

"Because I'd wait forever!" Faith sounded both angry and miserable. "Come on, Bonnie, you've seen Harald. He's positively gorgeous. And if I can't respond to him . . . well, then that makes me a hopeless case, doesn't it?" She sighed. "I've got a problem and I have to live with it. That's all."

"Nonsense," Bonnie said crisply. "Nick Justin got to you. It's written all over your face."

Faith opened her mouth to issue a denial, then stopped. "I did feel . . . different," she admitted. "But that doesn't mean anything."

"You've been kissing the wrong guy, Faith. Why won't you admit it? Harald may be well-endowed in the boyish charm department, but Nick Justin is a man."

"Oh, yes. He is that." Faith gulped some coffee and burnt her throat. "A man who hates me."

"I doubt that." Bonnie's smile insinuated quite the opposite, and Faith groaned in disgust.

"You didn't see his face when I left him on the platform."

"Neither did you," Bonnie protested. "You didn't have your glasses, remember?"

"I'll never see him again," Faith said firmly.

"Don't bet on it. If he's as mad as you say, he might just be mad enough to track you down."

Faith jumped at the thought. "No!"

"Yes. The court case, the *Newsview* story—that's plenty of motivation to go on searching for you. And if he's as intrepid as you say, he'll find you."

"Heaven help me," Faith said, "if he does."

4

⚬⚬⚬⚬⚬⚬⚬⚬⚬⚬

The story appeared in Monday morning's *New York Times*. The one-column item in the Metropolitan section began "Reporter Nabs Suspect on D Train; Mystery Woman Sought."

"Mystery Woman Sought." Faith's conscience jabbed her with needles of guilt. Of course, Nick could file charges on his own, and Nick's word would carry far more weight with a jury than hers ever could. But still, if that boy should get off—

Faith shook her head as if she could shake off her troubles. She had work to do. The Foundation's annual fundraising dinner-dance demanded her attention; if she wanted to get a feature piece to run in Friday's edition of *Newsday*, Faith had to turn in the copy this afternoon. Ordinarily, she could bang out a lively piece on the black-tie affair at the posh Tavern on the Green in a matter of minutes. Today, she pulled sheet after sheet out of the typewriter until the floor around her wastebasket was littered with crumpled paper macaroons.

Faith groaned. It did no good to stare at the blooming begonias hanging in her window when what she really needed was to talk to someone. She reached for the phone.

"Grossbaum and Smith."

"Attorney Smith, please. Faith Daniels calling."

In a moment Faith heard the reassuring gravelly voice of Mildred Smith. "Faith? What's up?"

"I'm in trouble, and I'd like to see you."

The phone was silent, as if the lawyer had to adjust to the idea of Faith being in the kind of trouble that would require her services. But the answering voice was as cool and nonjudgmental as ever. "Of course. Be glad to see you. How soon?"

"Do you have any free time today?"

"That bad, huh?" A brief pause. "Come right over."

"I don't mean to impose—I can wait—"

"Get your behind over here," was the affectionate reply.

Twenty minutes later Faith was ushered into the private office of Mildred Smith. The walnut furnishings and scarlet carpet were masculine in tone, but that was Mildred's own taste, not an inheritance from a former occupant. The office suited her, its no-nonsense furnishings a perfect reflection of the quality and intelligence of the woman behind the desk.

Mildred Smith was one of Faith's heroines. She'd worked for the Justice Department under Robert Kennedy and had also been a close friend of Faith's father and the first counsel to the Daniels Foundation. During the turmoil of the late sixties and early seventies, Mildred had served four terms in Congress, where her tart tongue and uncompromising principles had earned her a national reputation. Now she was a one-woman legal-aid service, even though she could have earned far more money serving the rich.

Mildred was in her sixties, a large-boned woman with iron-grey hair, a blustery manner and a face which made up in animation what it had always lacked in beauty.

"So, kid." She gestured Faith into a chair. "What's the problem? You get busted?"

Faith laughed. "Nothing so simple." She drew a deep breath. "Before I start, I need to be sure that you'll keep this absolutely confidential."

"You got it."

Faith told her story, from *Blood Poisoning*'s inception right up to Faith's appearance as the "Mystery Woman" in the *New York Times*. Mildred listened, but made no comment beyond an occasional raised eyebrow.

When Faith finished there was a long silence.

"So, kid. What do you want from me? Legal advice?"

Faith frowned. "How bad is it, ethically, if I don't go to the police?" she asked.

"I don't make moral judgments, Faith."

"But you have an opinion. As a friend."

"Okay. First things first. About your book. Good for you. Terrific." A grin cracked the edges of the stone face. "But how did you ever keep *Blood Poisoning* a secret from Prue?"

"I wrote it in Central Park, at the gazebo by the rowing pond. Longhand."

"My Lord." The lawyer shuddered—her handwritten labors were limited to scrawling her illegible signature at the bottom of checks. "Double that congratulations. Now for the unpleasant part."

Faith stared at the carpet. "You'd go to the police, wouldn't you?" she mumbled.

"Without batting an eyelash. But I'm not you, Faith. And I'm curious. You've always seemed to me to be, if anything, too scrupulous. Too careful. Too good for your own good, if you know what I mean."

"Boy, do I know what you mean." Faith grinned.

"In your case, a little adolescent rebellion is long overdue," Mildred said calmly. "But I don't know if you're asserting your independence and flouting the conventions, or if you're just scared stiff."

"At the moment, scared stiff." Faith laughed, but her eyes remained serious. "It's Prue. If she finds out about *Blood Poisoning*—"

"She won't like it."

"Won't like it?" Faith cried. "She'll drum me out of the family!"

"And would that be so terrible?"

"Of course! Prue is all I have."

Mildred looked at her closely. "Faith, child, being born a Daniels shouldn't seem like a life sentence without parole. Now, I know Prue can make leaving the Foundation sound like a capital crime—"

"High treason," Faith groaned. "And you know what the penalty for treason is."

"Did you ever ask yourself why she's so inflexible?" the lawyer continued. "You're probably the only kid in America who was never asked what she wanted to be when she grew up. Faith was always 'going into the Foundation.' Why?"

Faith was stunned to realize that Mildred's words were true; she took a long while to find an answer to the question. "Daddy, I guess," she said slowly. "For his sake. His work deserves to go on."

"For Harrison Daniels? Really?" Mildred paused. "Or for Prue?"

"For Prue?" Faith hesitated. "I don't understand."

"Think about her life. All she's ever had is Harry and his blasted Foundation. She's got no life of her own. No man, no kids. Even her dreams are secondhand."

"I guess that's why she wants me to follow in Daddy's footsteps."

Mildred snorted. "She doesn't want you to be just like Harry, damn it. She wants you to be just like *her.*"

Faith tried to protest but the words died on her lips. Just like Prue . . . what a horrible thought. And yet there was truth to what Mildred had said. Faith could feel it, like a cold worm crawling along her bones.

"If you become another old maid married to the Foundation," Mildred continued, "then you're saying that what Prue did with her life was right. If you insist on a different career, or a husband, kids, why then Prue has to question the choices she made. Maybe she could have had more, too. Why do you think she's fought so hard to keep you dependent on her? Shy and scared, with no mind of your own?"

Faith sat in silence while the grim implications of Mildred's words sank into her brain. She didn't want to accept the truth.

"Wait! You're wrong," Faith insisted. "Prue *wants* me to marry Harald. She pushed me into the engagement. Why, she and the Clintons were making wedding arrangements before I even said 'yes'!"

Mildred nodded. "And why does Prue want you to marry Harald, do you think?"

Faith thought of the peculiar, troubling alliance between her aunt and her fiancé: sometimes it seemed to Faith that Harald was far more interested in pleasing Prue than in pleasing her. "Because," she ventured, "Harald wants me tied to the Foundation just as much as Prue does?"

"Bingo." Mildred looked grim. "Clinton's a politician. He wants to keep you the ever-grieving child of the civil rights martyr, because that's where the votes are. He'll never condone you leaving the Foundation and disassociating yourself from your father's work."

"Oh, no," Faith cried.

"But surely you've guessed that?"

Faith hadn't wanted to think about it. Now she mumbled, "But that sounds like he just wants to use me."

"And you're too sweet to believe that." The lawyer sighed and got up from behind her desk. "Well, love is blind, they say. But remember—it's not disloyal to want a life of your own. Forget what Prue says. Your dad worked so that people could have more choices about what they did and how they lived. More freedom. Seems to me he'd want that freedom most of all for you."

Faith hugged Mildred and drew encouragement from her rocklike strength. Mildred would be on Faith's side, no matter what. "You've helped me so much," Faith told her.

"And what about this little police matter?" Mildred prompted.

Faith grimaced. "I guess I should file charges."

"I'll come with you, if that would help."

"I'll let you know. I won't go until after the big fundraiser Saturday night. I have a thousand things to do before then—"

"That's a pretty flimsy excuse, young lady."

"I know, but you know how Prue gets before fundraisers. If I have to tell her about the book, it'll be a lot easier next week."

"If you say so." Mildred paused. "Will you answer one question before you go?"

"Sure."

"What's between you and Nick Justin?"

Faith was startled. "Nothing," she stammered.

"Nothing. And she turns the color of a Harvard beet. Remind me never to put you on the stand in your own defense." Mildred chuckled. "Come on, tell me what you think of my buddy Nick."

"Your buddy?" Faith gasped incredulously.

"He's brought me some of my best cases," Mildred said. "He did two years at Columbia Law, you know."

"Nick Justin was one of your students?"

"Yep. The bar lost a great one when he turned to journalism."

"So that's where he learned cross-examination," Faith groaned. "I should have known."

"Tough, huh?"

"He cut me up in little pieces. By the time he was through I was so dizzy I hardly knew what I was saying."

"I can imagine." Mildred paused and eyed Faith shrewdly. "Have you slept with him yet?"

"God, no!"

"No need to sound so shocked, dear," Mildred said mildly. "People do it all the time. And it didn't take Sherlock Holmes to deduce that account of you two riding around the city was carefully edited."

Faith blushed. "He did . . . kiss me."

"Did he, indeed?" Mildred grinned. "He's a good man, Faith. Take my word."

"For crying out loud!" Faith protested with more vigor than necessary. "I'm engaged, remember?"

"To Jude Clinton's boy." Mildred sniffed. "And you know what the Clintons are. All show and no substance. No." She paused. "Justin's the man for you. And come to think of it"—her face grew thoughtful—"you might be just the right woman for him. A bit young, but maybe that's all to the good."

"How do you mean?" Faith asked, curious in spite of herself.

"He's been through a lot. It's made him damned cynical about life—and women in particular."

"I noticed," Faith said dryly.

"He's got his reasons. His divorce, and of course Cynthia's death has been a terrible burden—"

"His wife's dead?"

"Last winter. Her car went off the road up in the Catskills. Those mountain curves are treacherous even if you haven't been drinking, and of course, Cynthia, well . . . she had a problem." Mildred stopped short, as if reluctant to speak ill of the dead. "Lucky that little Becky wasn't in the car. But Nick blames himself."

"Why should he? It was an accident."

"Cynthia never drank until Nick's career skyrocketed," Mildred said bluntly. "That's when all their problems started. She thought she had to keep up with him, but she couldn't."

"She was famous in her own field," Faith argued.

"Wasn't enough. Not when her husband was a household word."

"So she drank."

"And . . . other things," Mildred said cryptically. "Nick's success was like poison to her. She lost confidence in her own work, spent all her time making him pay for what he'd done to her. Finally he gave up on the marriage and got a divorce. Way too late for his own good, if you ask me."

Faith shuddered. "You don't mean he still . . . loved her?"

"Oh, she stamped it out of him. Eventually. He hasn't been close to a woman since."

"How she must have hurt him," Faith whispered to herself, her face softening with compassion. She remembered the pain she'd noticed on Nick's face when he kissed her the first time, as if he dreaded his desire for her even as he felt it. As if he despised the vulnerability that could drive him to hold her, no matter how strongly his mind told him not to.

How much he must have loved Cynthia, Faith thought, to leave him so scarred.

"You might be just what he needs right now." Mildred's crisp, businesslike voice interrupted her thoughts.

"A little sweetness and innocence and trust could work wonders."

"Trust? Don't be silly," Faith exclaimed. "He'll never trust me after what I've done." Faith thought of the experiential gap between them, a gap far larger than their chronological ages. How could she begin to comprehend a man like Justin—much less gain his confidence—after her deceptions?

Mildred nodded happily, oblivious to Faith's concern. "Why, you're perfect for each other. You'd soften his bitterness, and he could toughen you up. Ideal." She smiled. "Some public-spirited citizen should give Nick a call and tell him where to find his Fanny Duvall."

"Mildred, no! You wouldn't!" Faith was frantic. "Promise me you won't tell him!"

"Of course I won't," Mildred said reassuringly, and eventually gave her word, but the lawyer's enigmatic smile lingered on Faith's mind for hours afterward. Was it a mistake to have confided in Mildred? she wondered. Mildred Smith hadn't risen to the top of her profession by being afraid to take matters into her own hands.

"Honey?" A voice penetrated the mists in Faith's mind. "What do you think?"

"What?" She looked up from her untouched dinner and saw Harald's frown. "I'm sorry. I've been distracted all evening, haven't I?"

"Is something wrong?" he asked.

Everything's wrong, Faith thought, but she shook her head. She had learned early in their relationship that there was no point in telling Harald Clinton her problems. She pictured those handsome blond brows drawing together, the chiseled mouth frowning at her. "Now, baby," he'd say, "you're getting all upset over nothing."

She gave her fiancé the answer he would understand. "Oh, a rough day at work. That's all."

Harald reached across and patted her hand, the hand with the shining diamond. "Now who's giving my baby a hard time?" He flashed the politician's smile she was beginning to despise.

"I interviewed a woman with a master's in social work." Faith sighed, remembering with fresh guilt the unpleasant hour. "She's in charge of a housing renovation project in the Bronx, and their funding's been cut as of the first of July."

"Too bad," Harald said mechanically.

"I felt terrible. I couldn't do a thing to help her."

"It's not your fault there's no money."

"Well, if it were just the money, I wouldn't feel so hypocritical."

"Hypocritical?" That got Harald's attention. "Why?"

"I couldn't help but think our positions should be reversed," Faith explained patiently. "With her qualifications and experience she should have my job. She's got ten years field experience—all I've got is a B.A. in English lit. So why am I Vice-President of the Daniels Foundation when she's out of work?"

"Because you're a Daniels." Harald laughed. "Why feel guilty about that? You work too hard as it is, trying to make up for the accident of birth. Just accept it, Faith. And relax. All work and no play—"

"Seriously, Harald—"

"Oh, all right, be serious, if we must." But his manner clearly stated that Faith was making a mountain out of a molehill. Faith began to seethe with frustration. When they'd first met, his politician's attentiveness had fooled her completely; she'd thought Harald considered her opinions important. Only recently had Faith detected, beneath the pose, the condescension.

"How would you feel," Faith ventured cautiously as she poked her dessert with a fork, "if I left the Foundation?"

"Well, I wouldn't expect you to hold more than a ceremonial post once we have kids. Wouldn't look right."

"What about before that? If I wanted to leave for, say, another career?"

"Another career?" Harald was astonished. "What else would you want to do?"

"Well, I've been thinking. . . ." Faith was suddenly afraid to broach the subject of her writing. She remembered the spirited defense of her work she'd flung at Nick Justin, and wondered. She hadn't been afraid to talk to *him*. Afraid of him, yes, maybe, but not afraid to be herself in front of him.

"You know," Faith said, with pretended casualness, "I've always loved to write."

"Of course you do, baby. Why, you've done a great job with the direct-mail campaign for the Foundation." Harald smiled and patted her hand. "Even Prue says so. I may need to put you to work on my campaign—"

"That isn't what I had in mind," Faith snapped. Harald looked offended, and Faith hastily pulled back from the brink of an argument. "It's . . . gratifying"—as she reached for all the tact in her system—"to feel that my letters might encourage people to give to a good cause. But what I really want to do is write fiction."

Harald seemed baffled. "You mean like short stories?"

"Novels, actually. My teachers all encouraged me—"

"Of course they did," Harald interrupted smoothly. "That's their job, honey. But just because you can write a good news release or a business letter doesn't mean you can write a book."

"It was just an idea," Faith muttered, sorry she had ever raised the subject.

He smiled again. "Hey, baby, if it makes you happy to scribble a few lines once in a while, then I say go ahead. But don't confuse that with your career. You're too valuable right where you are."

Valuable to whom? Faith wondered. To Harald Clinton? And conversely, perhaps a Daniels not tied to the Foundation was of no value to the aspiring Congressman. She bit her lip. Faith realized she'd been increasingly annoyed with Harald ever since the night of the Edgar banquet.

Or, to be precise, she'd been upset with Harald ever since she'd met Nick Justin. Even Harald's astonishing good looks had lost the power to charm her. His golden hair was as shiny as ever, his lake-blue eyes as dazzling. But when she contrasted Harald's perfect features with Nick Justin's rugged, intelligent face, Harald seemed insipid. Remote. A statue.

Whereas, Nick—Nick was undoubtedly alive. Electric. Challenging. And he never presumed her anything but his equal. Nick Justin had insulted her, yes, had baited Faith unmercifully. But always in his eyes was the glint which said, "We're in this together, and isn't it fun? See how much we can enjoy each other?"

Harald never looked at her that way, Faith realized now. Harald patronized her. Why on earth had she said she'd marry him?

It was not the first time she'd asked that question, but this time the answer startled her.

Gratitude. Because Harald wanted her, because Prue approved of him, because she felt so damn lucky to be asked.

Faith hadn't expected to marry at all. She'd seen herself wed to the Foundation, like her aunt. Now it struck her as rather odd that she'd so completely accepted Prue's image of her as dull, neuter. Maybe Faith was actually more like her mother, Cecily, the debutante who'd eloped at nineteen with a penniless preacher and so scandalized her Boston Brahmin family that they'd disinherited her. Cecily Cobb Daniels had gone to Mississippi with her husband and never looked back.

Harrison's murder had devastated Cecily, shattered her gentle soul. She'd survived her husband by less than two years. And her young daughter was left to Prudence Daniels to raise. Sometimes Faith feared she was just as unable to deal with life's harsh realities as Cecily had been. She'd inherited her mother's looks, why not her romantic soul as well?

No wonder she'd chosen to identify with Prue. Sexless, drab, dutiful Prue, who never expected much from life and was never disappointed.

"We have to set a date for the wedding, you know." Harald's voice intruded into her thoughts. "The end of September?"

"Won't that take time from the campaign?" Faith asked absently.

"Well, I thought of waiting until after the election, but the publicity we'd get if we marry during the campaign is just too good to pass up. Of course, I'll have to curtail my schedule for a few days."

"I should hope so," Faith remarked.

"But the honeymoon can wait until after Election Day. If you don't mind."

"I don't mind." She'd expected that. Romance would always run second to politics where a Clinton was concerned.

"Then it's settled."

They left the restaurant and walked in silence down Columbus Avenue toward Faith's apartment. Faith felt suddenly and inexplicably sad. Come fall, she would be Mrs. Harald Clinton. Why did that depress her? When Harald had proposed it had seemed so marvelous! Faith hadn't been swept off her feet with passion, exactly, but she'd been convinced she couldn't be, so what did it matter? Harald was clever and ambitious; he fit easily into her world, and she cherished a secret hope of doing some good in his. And, of course, there would be children. . . .

Faith often daydreamed of the children she would have with Harald, blond children with laughing faces. Lately, more and more, those dreams were of children with disturbing hazel eyes and tousled hair.

Nick Justin again. Faith groaned, choked back a caustic comment she was about to make regarding Harald's campaign strategy, and led the way into her apartment.

Bonnie was out. Nervously, Faith flipped on the lights, dreading what would happen next.

She and Harald had been lovers since their engagement, a circumstance which brought Faith mixed emotions. The actual lovemaking she found pleasant enough, but she'd always suspected she could—and should—feel more than she did, and wondered whether there was something wrong with her.

Now those vague doubts had crystalized into concrete fear: that there was something amiss in the relationship that would not be mended by time, experience or wedding vows.

Faith kept remembering, with acute discomfort, what she had felt when Nick Justin kissed her.

Bonnie had been right when she'd said that Nick Justin had changed Faith; he'd made her aware that she was capable of a far greater intensity of sexual feeling than she'd ever dreamed. Ever since that night, she'd busied herself trying to find a rationalization for her response, some innocent explanation that didn't have anything to do with the man himself.

Faith had decided that she was simply blooming. Ripening, like fruit on a tree. And Nick Justin had simply been there at the right time.

Now, surely, Faith could feel that heightened response with any man. Certainly with Harald.

But she didn't.

Faith stalled her way through a tortuous half-hour of foreplay on the couch, hoping madly that her nervous embarrassment would vanish and the magic would take hold. But after telling herself a thousand and one private lies, Faith admitted the truth.

She didn't want Harald. At all.

Well, maybe if she pretended he was Nick—

No. Impossible.

She could remember Nick too well, and simply to recall the sensual movement of his lips, the teasing intimacy of his hands, made her insides shriek with longing.

Oh, Faith had changed, all right, but not in the way she had hoped. Nick Justin had not thrown a switch inside her enabling her to respond to any attractive man; he had claimed her for his own as surely as if he'd put a brand on her.

Damn, she thought, as she twisted away from Harald's grasp and saw the questioning look in his eyes. This was worse than she'd thought. She no longer found Harald's lovemaking tolerably pleasant, as before. Now she felt disappointed and depressed and used. At his suggestion that they abandon the couch for her bedroom, Faith felt a distaste bordering on revulsion.

"I . . . can't," she mumbled. She pulled away and began to rebutton her blouse.

"What are you talking about?" Harald pulled her back against him, his voice lazy and utterly confident. "Sweetheart—"

"No. I mean it." Faith rose from the couch and strode across the narrow living room toward the door. "I'd like you to leave. I'm sorry," she added in a softer tone, as she saw the puzzlement on his face. "I'm just not feeling well, I guess."

"Oh. Well. Okay." Harald could accept the neutral

excuse. Faith cringed to think of his reaction if she told
him the truth. When at last she closed the door behind
him, after a final proprietary embrace, Faith was shaking,
but not with passion.

With fear. She couldn't marry Harald Clinton.

Somehow, she was going to have to find a way to
break the engagement—without bruising Harald's ego or
ruffling Prue's feathers or arousing anyone's suspicions
about her change of heart. But how?

That night Faith tossed and turned for hours, but
couldn't come up with one helpful idea. And when at last
she slept, she dreamt of Nick Justin.

As the week dragged on, Faith grew more and more
restless. This was a time of peak activity for the Foundation as Saturday's fundraising dance approached, yet
Faith remained aloof from the hyperactivity in the office
and the bustle of preparations at Tavern on the Green.
Even Prue's bald announcement that her niece would
have to make an after-dinner speech left Faith unmoved.
She couldn't seem to concentrate on anything but Nick
Justin. Faith was dismayed at how often the reporter, as
arrogant in mind as he was in person, slipped into her
thoughts.

Even her favorite retreat brought her no peace. Faith
always went to the gazebo in Central Park when she was
troubled. She'd stretch out on one of the hard wooden
benches and gaze across the rowing pond to the out-
spread skyline of Manhattan. The rolling water and
swaying willows never failed to soothe her.

Until now.

On Friday morning Faith came to the gazebo at
sunrise, a ritual she'd observed daily for almost three
years. The dinner-dance was a day away, but Faith had
made no progress on her speech. Now a blank legal pad
lay across her lap. She tried to concentrate.

"Thanks a bundle, Aunt Prue," she muttered.

No words came. Instead, an inscrutable hazel-eyed face swam before her vision.

Figaro, Faith's Old English sheepdog, tried to climb into Faith's lap and distract her. She rubbed his neck.

Footsteps echoed on the path which led down from the road, quickly followed by a familiar voice. "How's it going?"

"Lousy." Faith waved at the uniformed policeman. "Hi, Joe."

"Hi. Hi, Figaro." He petted the dog enthusiastically. "You want me to walk Figaro around for a bit? Take him off your hands?"

"That'd be great." Every morning the beat cops checked on Faith with clocklike regularity, and usually they'd take Figaro on part of their patrol. Faith found the protective attitude of the police at once amusing and reassuring. She wore a whistle around her neck to summon help in case of trouble, but had never had to use it.

"You're losing weight," Joe said critically. "Maybe I should bring you back a danish? Or a bagel?"

"No, thanks. I've been a little upset, that's all."

Joe's level gaze took her in from head to toe. "Man trouble?" he asked.

"And they talk about women's intuition." Faith laughed. "I'd take a cop's intuition any day."

"Problems with Harald?"

"No. Not really." Faith screwed up her face against the morning sunlight, and looked at Joe. His six-foot-three-inch frame nearly reached the cupola roof of the gazebo. "Joe," she asked, "how do you know when you're in love?"

Joe, six years married and father of two, smiled broadly. "Sure and it's a funny time for you to be asking that, Faith, and you engaged for weeks."

"I know," Faith fretted. "But how *do* you know? And don't say 'You just know.' That's no help."

"You feel different. Like your body was on low speed and suddenly kicked into high. Now me, I was dizzy. Couldn't sleep. And believe it or not," he said, patting his slight paunch, "I started skipping meals."

Faith laughed again.

"All I wanted to talk about was Sharon, see. And if I couldn't talk about her, I was sure enough thinking about her." The policeman leaned forward. "Sound familiar?"

"I'm afraid so," Faith admitted.

Joe looked at Faith's legal pad, its top page now covered with cross-outs and false starts. "By the look of that, I'd say you got it bad." He grinned again. "Congratulations."

"Congratulations my foot," Faith yelled as Joe picked up Figaro's leash and led the dog away. "He's arrogant and impossible! And besides, I'll never see him again."

The cop grinned. "Would you like to make a small bet?"

"I would not."

"Ah, darling. Love is grand," Joe teased. "Why fight it?"

Those words raced around Faith's mind long after Joe and Figaro disappeared in the trees. In love? With Nick? She couldn't be. She scarcely knew Nick Justin. The sparks they'd struck from the moment of meeting must be sheer sexual attraction, temporarily devastating to Faith because she'd never felt it before, but nothing more.

Yet Faith half wished she'd told Mildred Smith that she could tip Justin off to Fanny Duvall's true identity. Then, at least, Faith might see him again.

To Faith's surprise, her speech went well. The lavish meal and elegant surroundings of Tavern on the Green

perhaps predisposed her audience to approve her re-
marks. Afterwards, she retreated to the ladies' lounge
and sat in front of the mirror while her pulse returned to
normal.

Faith hated these Foundation-sponsored social events;
they always depressed her. The guests inevitably stared
at her as if she were a museum exhibit, and Faith never
felt free to be herself.

"Faith? Are you in here?" Bonnie's voice rang out.

"Sorry," Faith grumbled. "I got tired of being on
display."

"No wonder. You'd think you were running for office
instead of Harald." Bonnie grimaced and shook out the
ruffles of her gown. "But come back now. The band's
starting."

"In a minute." Faith inexpertly put drops in her eyes
and smeared her makeup.

"Are those new contacts bothering you?"

"Just a bit," Faith admitted. "They dry out—all the
smoke, I think." After the debacle at the Edgar banquet,
Faith had invested in soft contact lenses, determined
never to sacrifice her vision to her vanity again.

Bonnie paced the small lounge, her full-skirted dress
swinging. The green chiffon fabric had a silver thread in
the weave so that she seemed to sparkle as she walked.
Faith noted that the sparkle was not confined to Bonnie's
dress; her eyes gleamed with mischief.

"What's got into you?" Faith demanded. "You look
like the cat that swallowed the canary."

"Oh, it's the music," Bonnie said glibly. "And the
atmosphere. Everyone looks so glamorous. I feel so
romantic, if Gilbert proposes again I might say yes."

Bonnie's rejections of long-suffering Gilbert were leg-
endary. "I'll believe that when you walk down the aisle,"
Faith said dryly.

"Shall I fix your eyes?" Bonnie offered as Faith squinted and dabbed at her makeup.

"Would you please?"

Bonnie busied herself with soft lilac powder and brush. "I thought you might be sulking."

"Why?"

"To spite Prue," Bonnie said frankly. "For whisking Harald out from under your nose. You'd think he was engaged to her, the way she's paraded around with him all night! Why doesn't he tell her to buzz off?"

"Bad politics. Never cross a person with power."

"Well, he's making enough points tonight," Bonnie commented. "But then, marrying Harrison Daniels' only daughter isn't going to hurt him with this crowd."

Faith knew she was expected to defend her fiancé's behavior, but her patience was exhausted. She sighed. "Oh, Bonnie."

"Don't 'Oh, Bonnie' me. Here. How's that?"

Faith's eyes looked gigantic, the skillful lilac shadow bringing unaccustomed drama to her Madonna-like face. She had her long hair styled in a Gibson, with tendrils escaping about her cheeks and neck. And her dress was simply the most elegant gown she'd ever owned. The strapless pink silk sheath had tiny crosswise tucks in the bodice and about the hem. The dress showed off Faith's beautiful shoulders and her slim silhouette to perfection.

"My God," Bonnie said reverently, "you look like Garbo."

Faith laughed nervously and rose. She had never been comfortable accepting compliments. "It's the dress. And the hairdo."

"It's your face. And your shoulders. And what are you doing with that?"

Bonnie snatched the short-sleeved bolero jacket out of Faith's hands. Faith had worn the gown's matching jacket all evening, feeling the strapless look too daring for the founder's baby girl.

"You aren't going to put that on again."

"Why not?" Faith asked.

"Faith. Be real. Show off a little."

Faith blushed and looked in the mirror at the expanse of creamy flesh showing above the bodice of her gown, at her throat set off with a delicate amethyst necklace that had been Cecily's. "I can't," she protested. "Aunt Prue would have a coronary if I walked out there like this."

Bonnie sniffed. "Let her eat her heart out. You're beautiful, Faith—flaunt it for once. Men will throw themselves at your feet, I guarantee it."

Faith hesitated. "You don't think the dress is too . . . revealing?"

"Have you seen some of the women out there, Faith? This is positively tame! And very classy." Bonnie grinned and clutched the pink jacket. "I'll take this back and put it on your chair."

"Don't be silly. I'm perfectly capable of carrying my own jacket. You're my friend, not my maid."

"I insist," Bonnie said.

Faith rose. "Okay, let's go."

"No." Bonnie moved swiftly. "Give me a minute. You should make your own entrance. This is your party."

"Don't be silly," Faith protested, but Bonnie was adamant. "Someone wants to see you privately and he won't appreciate my tagging along." And with a broad wink, Bonnie left.

Faith knew herself no match for Bonnie's stubbornness, so she sat quietly for a moment and wondered what her friend was up to. Probably Harald would be waiting in the foyer to escort Faith out into the moonlight for a spot of romance.

Faith walked out into the wood-paneled reception area. Ahead lay the Elm Room, and beyond it, the private dining room set aside for the Foundation. Faith could hear an alto sax moaning a bittersweet Gershwin melody.

A waiter balancing a loaded tray caught sight of Faith and stopped dead, nearly dropping his dishes into a diner's lap.

Faith hid a smile. Bonnie must be right about the dress.

As Faith squeezed past the hapless waiter, a hand touched her bare back. This must be Bonnie's surprise, she thought, and whirled around as a voice spoke.

"Fanny Duvall!"

The voice belonged to Nick Justin.

5

*《******※*

You!" Faith gasped, rather as Eve must have greeted the serpent in the Garden of Eden.

Nick Justin's hazel-green eyes gleamed like the coals of a dead fire. "Astute as ever, Fanny," he drawled.

"Don't call me Fanny!"

"Why ever not?" Nick asked, challenging her.

"You know why. And keep your voice down." Faith looked down the length of the Elm Room. How long could she stand here before someone she knew came by and called her name?

"You're impossible," Faith hissed.

"But persistent."

"I noticed." Her arm, beneath Nick's clenched fingers, grew numb. "What are you going to do?" she demanded.

Nick didn't answer. His eyes raked Faith's body, from the top of her Gibson knot to the slit skirt which revealed a slim calf and ankle. Nick's eyes returned, not to her face, but to the top of her strapless gown, as if he were fascinated by the line of her neck and shoulders, the hint of the cleft between her breasts.

Faith blushed. If only she had her demure pink jacket! Blast Bonnie and her helpful ideas.

"Let go of me!" she cried in a whisper.

"No chance. I made that mistake once. Believe me, never again." He smiled down at her, a smile Faith thought showed a touch of cruelty. "You keep watching that door. That's the Daniels Foundation party, isn't it? Why don't we go down there and get better acquainted. . . ."

"No!" If they walked into that room, Faith's secret was out. Not only would Nick learn who she was, but he would tell Prue and Harald and anyone else who'd listen that Faith had deceived them all. That she had another life as author Fanny Duvall, and probably a string of lovers, too. Trust Justin to throw that in. . . .

"You're pale, Fanny," Nick said. "Why?"

Faith made a helpless gesture that indicated problems too vast for words to encompass. "What do you want?"

"All you have to offer," Nick replied, "but let's start with an explanation of why you left me on that station platform alone, with two cops who were convinced the hotshot reporter was pulling a practical joke on them. You at least owe me that much."

Faith's inbred sense of fair play agreed that Nick deserved an explanation. But how much longer could they stand together in the foyer before gossip started? Already the coatroom attendant was staring at them—

"Not tonight," she whispered breathlessly. "Tomorrow. I'll meet you. Anywhere you say. But—"

"No way. Here and now, Fanny."

"I can't!" Faith looked again over her shoulder, down the Elm Room aisles. Was that Harald who stood in the open doorway? "Not here," she begged.

"Outside, then. Come on."

"Please, can't you—"

"You've got no choice." His hand slid roughly down her left arm to pull her after him. Nick stopped short. His eyes jerked up to meet Faith's. His fingers rotated her diamond solitaire, the ring she hadn't worn the night of the Edgar awards. "What's this? Engaged?" His eyebrows lifted. "Don't tell me Powell got his divorce so soon?"

"Not Ken Powell," she snapped angrily.

"I thought not. So you've bagged yourself a sucker, have you? Well, let's go meet the future Mr. Duvall. I'd enjoy that."

The unspoken threat hung in the air. "You skunk!" Faith whispered.

"We've got a lot to discuss, he and I."

"That's blackmail."

"Damn right," Nick retorted. "Tell me what I want to know or we march into that party and you can spill your guts in front of your intended. You decide."

Faith conceded defeat. "Outside," she hissed, "and be discreet, if that word's in your vocabulary."

"I'll look it up." Nick propelled her firmly out the front door.

Well, at least half the restaurant staff saw that, Faith thought. If Harald asked questions, a dozen people could say where the girl in the pink dress had gone—and with whom.

She picked her way dejectedly through the parked cars bordered by Central Park.

"You're not afraid to be at my mercy in the dark?"

"I've been at your mercy in worse places," Faith muttered as they stopped by a park bench. Nick laughed softly.

"And your fiancé won't be upset to find you out in the

moonlight with another man? Or is the poor guy used to it by now?"

"There's no need to be so offensive."

"Oh, no, let's be civilized and proper. You're always proper, aren't you, Fanny? Except for bothering to spend a few minutes with the police—"

"I said I'm sorry—"

"Sure you are. God, I'll never forget how you skipped across that platform as gay as you please while I tried to explain where the star witness was going. It would've been downright comical if that kid wasn't dangerous—"

"I'm sorry," Faith repeated, guilt-stricken. "I wanted to stay."

"But Ken Powell was waiting for you. I know. Oh, I was welcome enough when I saved you," Nick continued bitterly. "But the minute you could ditch me for your lover—"

"So that's it!" Faith cried. "I've dented your colossal ego. Well, excuse me. I suppose I could apologize for a century and it wouldn't be enough."

"Don't waste your words on me," Nick snapped. "I could care less. My ego's been bruised by experts and survived. Just march yourself down to the precinct and swear out a complaint against that punk. Right now."

Faith's jaw dropped. "You're crazy! How can I?"

"Easy. Just put one foot in front of another."

"Don't you understand? I want to see that kid convicted. Believe me," Faith said earnestly. "I feel horrible that I can't go to the police. But I can't. There are reasons. . . ."

"Oh, you've always got your reasons, haven't you?" His voice was harsh. "Find the next woman who gets on a train with that kid and has nobody around to help her. You go tell her your reasons."

Nick's anger surprised Faith. He could laugh off her

slight to his ego, his personal embarrassment, but he was furious that she would endanger her fellow man.

"I am so sorry," Faith said, and her tone was chastened this time. "You don't know what it means to be scared, so maybe you can't understand how I feel. To know that someone else might get hurt because I was a coward."

"You admit it?" Nick demanded, surprised.

"Of course. But I ran because I was afraid, not to punish you. I'm not like that."

"I see," he said, and some of the anger had gone out of his face. "Afraid of what?"

"Of you," Faith said reluctantly. "Fanny Duvall isn't my real name. You know that. I couldn't tell the police who I really was, and where I lived, without you finding out, and . . . using it against me."

Nick stopped pacing the sidewalk in front of the bench and dropped down at Faith's side. "You might as well tell me now," he said abruptly. "You know I'll find out anyway."

"I know you will." She sighed. He had won. He always won. She looked up at Nick's face, but saw no gloating over her predicament, simply honest curiosity and a softer emotion that might have been concern.

"My name," she said slowly, "is Faith Daniels."

His eyebrows shot up. "Not Harrison Daniels' daughter?"

So he hadn't guessed. Faith nodded, and felt a weight passing out of her conscience.

"But—" A series of emotions passed over Nick's face: shock, incredulity, compassion, puzzlement. "I thought you were just a little girl!"

"I'm twenty-three."

"Son of a gun. Time flies." His hand made an absent pass across his forehead, brushing his thick hair back from his eyes. "Of course, we never really get over losing a man like Harrison Daniels. Maybe that's what keeps it fresh in the mind."

Faith, who could have borne Nick's cynicism with equanimity, felt embarrassed by his sympathetic tone. She struggled against tears.

"Is it as bad as that?" Somehow his arm had come around her shoulders.

"You can't imagine."

"Tell me," he said gently.

And she did—told him everything. The words cascaded like water over a dam. Words about Prue, the Foundation, her book, the deception that had grown out of control. When she had finished, she felt soothed. Cleansed.

"Poor Fanny. You've never had a soul to call your own, have you? But don't worry about being a coward. To write that book took guts."

"That comes and goes," Faith said ruefully, "but thanks." Somehow her head nestled comfortably against Nick's shoulder. "Have you met my Aunt Prue?"

"Yep."

"And what do you think?"

"She has all the sensitivity of a steel corset and the charm of a barrel of brine."

Faith laughed, then shushed herself. "She'll take a whip to me if she finds out about *Blood Poisoning*. Or worse. Maybe boot me out of the family for good."

"Ah, yes, the Foundation adopts a rather strident moral tone these days, doesn't it? I wonder what Harrison Daniels would think?"

"He'd hate it," Faith said firmly. "Daddy tried to help people, not judge them. Prue's different. She likes power, to control other people's lives."

"Starting with yours?" Nick asked shrewdly.

"You know it."

"What about your fiancé, whoever he is? Won't he support you?"

"Harald?" Faith shuddered. "Are you kidding? He'll hand Prue the stones to throw at me."

Nick offered a profane assessment of Harald's character that Faith rather enjoyed.

"He doesn't love me," Faith explained in a choked voice. "Not the real me, the scruffy, blunt, profane me. He loves Harrison Daniels' sweet hypocritical daughter."

"So you're not the same person your dad was," Nick retorted. "That's no crime. So you're not the woman Prudence Daniels wants you to be. If you ask me, that's a blessing."

Faith laughed. "Does that mean I'm forgiven my sins?"

"No."

Faith did a double take as she realized Nick was serious. "But what else do you want from me?"

"This, for a start." He narrowed the gap between her lips and his and brushed her mouth with the gentlest of kisses. Faith's pulse fluttered and she leaned toward him. Nick placed his hands on either side of her neck and kissed her repeatedly, soft, teasing kisses that simultaneously promised yet withheld satisfaction. Each kiss tempted her closer, built her hunger for him. Faith's hands slipped around his waist.

She whispered his name in an odd, uncontrolled voice. He brushed a finger across her parted lips.

"First, promise."

"Anything," she murmured automatically.

"Go to the police and swear out a complaint against that boy. It won't take much of your time."

Faith turned numb. Go to the police. Press charges. All his kisses were nothing but sweet manipulation to persuade her to do what he wanted. A wave of humiliation engulfed Faith. When she thought how she'd nearly blurted out her desire for him, and all Nick was thinking of was business! Faith pulled herself out of his arms with some indignation.

"You needn't resort to seduction," she snapped.

"Oh, is that what I was doing?"

"It's my duty to go and I will." Pride made her voice stiff. "I give you my word of honor."

"Honor?" he asked dubiously. "You?"

Faith choked back a curse. "You are the most exasperating, maddening man, and you can go to hell!"

Nick laughed. He'd been teasing her, Faith realized, and she sputtered at him angrily. Nick caught her arm and pulled her down on the bench, nearly onto his lap. His hazel eyes blazed as his lips drew close to hers. Absorbed in each other, neither heard the approaching footsteps.

"Faith?" called a male voice. "Is that you?"

"Harald!" She jumped out of Nick's arms.

"What's going on here?"

Faith's mind raced. There must be a plausible explanation for her being with Nick—but what?

Nick negated Faith's efforts to look innocent by placing his arm protectively around her shoulder. She shot Nick a furious glance, but his eyes were on Harald as if taking the other man's measure.

This can't be happening, Faith thought. In a moment they'll bare teeth and growl like bulldogs. She studied the men: Harald, taller, rangier, his blond hair greyed by the moonlight; Nick, solid, tough, forthright, his athletic body accented by his formal attire rather than disguised by it.

Faith recalled her first impression of Nick Justin: formidable. Perhaps her fiancé was having the same reaction. The belligerence on Harald's aristocratic face faded to a sulk as he decided not to challenge the reporter.

"Harald, you recognize Nick Justin, surely," Faith

purred in her most civilized tone. "We've been discussing Daddy. Nick, this is Harald Clinton, my fiancé."

"A pleasure," Harald said, in a tone that indicated the opposite. "I'd've thought Harrison Daniels was a bit before your time."

"I didn't know him professionally," Nick replied smoothly. "But I admired him."

"And his daughter." Harald made the words an accusation.

"Doesn't everyone?" Nick's voice seemed to chop several feet off Harald's stature. "My congratulations."

"Thanks." Harald reached for Faith and put a proprietorial arm around her. "I think we'd better go circulate, honey."

"Mustn't neglect those voters," Nick added. "Right, Clinton?"

Harald flushed. "Faith's place is at the party," he said defensively. "She's Vice-President of the Foundation, you know."

"Really? She didn't mention that. A woman of many talents, it would appear."

Faith's heart stopped. Nick wouldn't dare mention her book . . . would he? "Please," she muttered. "You're embarrassing me."

"Modest to a fault," Nick went on. "Really, Clinton, you've no idea what a treasure you've got there."

"I know all there is to know about Faith," Harald said flatly, and Faith flinched. The challenge in his tone was unmistakable.

Nick let it pass. "Of course," Nick said. "When's the happy day?"

"We haven't set a date," Faith said in a rush. "What with Harald's campaign and all—"

"Ah, yes, first things first," Nick said, and went on to make barbed observations about Harald's campaign.

The friction between the two men had not abated by the time they entered the party, and Nick showed no sign of being ready to make a polite disappearance.

"Harald, let's dance," Faith said in desperation. "Nice to see you," she muttered to Nick, and rushed out onto the dance floor.

While Harald guided her rather stuffily around the floor, his displeasure evident, Faith's eyes followed Nick. When he joined Mildred Smith, Faith groaned inwardly.

Mildred. Of course. The lawyer had kept her word not to divulge that Faith was Fanny Duvall; she'd merely enticed Nick to the fundraiser and let nature take its course.

Caught by a technicality, Faith thought, and made a mental note to harangue Mildred about the lawyer's devious mind.

"Hey. Wake up." Harald's annoyance was plain. "What's the matter with you tonight?"

"Just exhausted," she lied, and added, "It's a strain to mingle and shake hands all night."

"You'd better get used to it," he replied. "You've signed on for a lifetime of it, remember."

Faith had a sudden vision of what Harald saw as her future, and cringed. A meek and polite woman in a sea of strangers, she would sing Harald's praises, make herself useful, and have a plate of hot hors d'oeuvres permanently affixed to her left hand.

"No," Faith said aloud.

"No what?" Harald smiled indulgently at her.

How insipid he looks, she thought. How had she ever thought Harald so handsome? There was no strength in that face, no uncommon intelligence, no compassion.

Just then Faith chanced to catch sight of Nick Justin; he was deep in conversation and gesturing emphatically. Even from across the room she felt the force of his personality, and found herself wishing, rather wistfully, that she were in the knot of people standing around Nick instead of dancing with Harald.

"Faith!" A piercing voice shattered Faith's thoughts. "Where's your jacket? You certainly don't intend to parade around the room half-naked?"

"This is hardly half-naked, Aunt Prue." Prudence Daniels never approved of a dress unless it had long sleeves and a Peter Pan collar.

"You look like a harlot," Prue insisted. Her own grey dress was high-necked and long-sleeved and without adornment. The plain square watch she wore, on a black leather band, could scarcely qualify as jewelry.

Faith sighed. Even the folds of material could not give her aunt an illusion of softness: Prue was a sharp-faced, sharp-voiced woman, her body all acute angles and bones. She was a little over medium height but painfully thin, and her steel-framed glasses made her blue eyes look even smaller. Faith often thought Prue looked like a woman whose femininity had been siphoned off, leaving a brittle, dried-up shell.

A fear of becoming like that had driven Faith into Harald's arms.

"Cover yourself up," Prue continued. "And fix your lipstick. Do you want the whole city to know you've been kissing and carrying on? It's time you acted like your father's daughter!"

There it was, the endless refrain. Faith bit her lip. She never had an answer for that.

Harald shifted his weight from one foot to the other. He never interfered between Faith and her aunt. Faith gave him an irritated glance and turned away.

"Don't you leave without answering me, miss." Prue jabbed a long finger at Faith's retreating back.

Faith didn't notice. She stood transfixed and watched in horror as Nick Justin approached. What if he intended

to make trouble? Nick hadn't promised to keep her
secret. Hadn't promised anything. Faith's heart began to
pound.

"My heavens. Nick Justin. Here." Prue's voice took on
an unaccustomed flutter of nervousness. "He can't be
investigating the Foundation, can he? Our reputation has
always been above reproach."

"Relax. He's here socially," Harald said. "Isn't he,
Faith?"

"How would she know?" Prue demanded.

Harald sounded displeased. "They're acquainted."

"Surely not." Prue gave a deprecating laugh.

"We met briefly," Faith explained hurriedly, then
added, "Mr. Justin is a great admirer of Daddy."

"Oh," Prue said, satisfied, and let the subject drop.
That the reporter should admire her brother was only
natural; that he might admire her niece was beyond the
bounds of probability.

Faith grew annoyed. Why was it that lately everything
her aunt said raised her hackles? When Nick approached,
Faith performed the introductions, and a devil inside
Faith wanted to make more of her relationship with Nick
than actually existed, just to confound Prue and Harald.

The conversation stayed bland and neutral: Nick's
latest stories, the economy, government cutbacks. Prue
insinuated, more than once, that a *Newsview* story on the
Foundation—favorable, of course—might help bring in
much-needed contributions. Faith blushed for her aunt,
whose single-mindedness was more obvious and embarrassing than usual. And Harald, ever the aspiring
Congressman, lost no opportunity to emphasize his
credentials.

Faith squirmed with embarrassment. She dared not try
to steer the conversation to livelier topics, lest she skate
too near her personal life and risk exposure. She must
stay mute and endure Prue's self-centered musings and

Harald's shameless politicking. Faith looked at Nick with helpless apology.

Humor danced in his hazel-green eyes. He disengaged Prue's arm with brisk efficiency.

"I see the orchestra is back. Would you like to dance, Miss Daniels?"

Faith gasped. Prue's reaction was stronger: she laughed aloud. "Faith never dances," she declared. "Except with her fiancé."

"Of course she does," Nick said easily. "I've seen her."

At the Edgar banquet. In Ken Powell's arms. A chill blew across Faith's heart. If Nick said anything about that night. . . .

She saw his strategy then. She could refuse to dance, and risk his mentioning the banquet, or she could agree, and face Prue and Harald's questions afterward. She was damned either way.

Well, then, she might as well do as she pleased. She recalled the feeling of Nick's arms around her, so long ago in the cab, and Harald and Prue were forgotten. "I'd love to dance," she murmured defiantly, and took Nick's hand.

The dance had a Latin rhythm, unfamiliar to Faith, but after her initial panic she gave herself over to the movements of Nick's body and managed to follow him quite creditably. The hectic movement brought color to her cheeks and her eyes sparkled; the tension slowly ebbed from her body. She looked up at Nick and he laughed aloud.

"That's better," he said. "I thought it was about time I rescued you."

"I wanted to rescue you! I was afraid you would be bored to death!"

"Forget it." He grinned, dismissing the awkward moments as if they'd never existed. "Half the people I meet want to get on my show, the other half want to get off it."

"Still, thanks for not giving me away."

"The night is young," Nick replied.

Faith nearly choked. "You wouldn't!"

"That all depends," he said silkily. "What kind of bribe are you offering?" And his strong hands pulled Faith closer, until her hips pressed into his and she felt his motion through her whole body.

Her temperature shot up. Her body melted against him. "Good girl," he whispered, his mouth against her ear. He kept her close, dancing with an intimacy Faith found shocking and marvelous and altogether wicked.

As a couple, they attracted attention. Faith caught Mildred Smith's quick cat-and-canary smile, and when Bonnie recognized Faith's partner her eyes grew wide as saucers. Harald, far from pleased, glared at Faith nonstop and paced erratically at the edge of the crowd.

"Your fiancé looks a bit upset," Nick murmured.

"Do you wonder why?" Faith asked, as Nick's hand briefly cupped her bottom, then slid slowly up along her hip. "Are you deliberately trying to provoke him?"

"Maybe I'm trying to provoke you. Or are you too scared of me to protest?"

"No," Faith admitted, "but stop."

"Yes, ma'am." He smiled down at her, content, his eyes more green than Faith had ever seen them. "You're a lovely partner, Fanny."

She tensed. "Don't call me Fanny."

"It just slipped out."

"Like your hand just slipped down."

"That was intentional. Temptation too great to resist. The rest of you is so slender—" He murmured a simile that made her face flame. Faith felt suddenly out of her depth.

"Don't talk like that," she whispered, embarrassed.

"Why not?"

"Anyone might hear."

"Has anyone ever told you that you worry a damn sight too much about what other people think?"

"You don't understand," she hissed. "You're a man." He grinned. "You noticed."

"You make it hard to think of anything else," Faith muttered, not for him to hear.

Nick laughed softly. "You know, I believe that's the first compliment you ever paid me."

"And the last," she retorted, angry that she'd betrayed her attraction to him.

"Promises, promises." Nick's fingers traced a pattern across her bare shoulder. His touch was moth-light, scarcely a caress at all, yet it went through Faith like a flame. "Where's the faithful fiancé, I wonder?" he asked. "He should be breathing fire by now."

"I . . . don't know." She didn't want to discuss Harald.

"Come on, Fanny." Nick's voice hardened. "He's mad as hell, but he won't cut in because that might offend me. And if he offended me, that might hurt his campaign. Isn't it nice to know where you stand in Harald Clinton's grand scheme of things? Somewhere below the ballot box?"

"I've always known," Faith said, and tried to look as if she didn't care. "I'm used to it."

Nick cursed with surprising violence. "Don't be a fool," he said roughly. "You deserve better."

Faith had no answer for that, so they finished the dance in strained silence. When Nick left her, she felt strangely bereft, even though Harald appeared almost immediately to lead her back onto the dance floor.

The music was slow, a torchy ballad; Harald ground his body against Faith's as if determined to assert his ownership. Guiltily, Faith acquiesced, but more and more Harald's body felt like a weapon used against her, and she resented his proprietary touch.

How she wished she were anywhere but in his arms! Frustrated, she closed her eyes and thought instead of Nick—his infuriating, perplexing behavior, his unexpected concern.

"You are so gorgeous tonight." Harald was breathing heavily, his mouth hovering next to Faith's ear. "I can't wait to take you home to bed. How soon can we get out of here?"

"What?" Faith had only half heard him. "We can't leave for hours, Harald. We're the hosts, remember?"

"Damn," he said softly.

Faith saw his eyes then, and jolted with alarm. Harald pulled her back against him, muttering about how much he wanted her until Faith thought she would scream.

Make love to Harald? Faith's mind balked at the thought. Not again, she whispered to herself, and then, frighteningly, *not ever.*

There it was, cold hard truth. She couldn't marry Harald, no matter what he wanted, no matter how much it would please Aunt Prue. She would have to find a way to stand up for herself, break the engagement, be done with this charade.

Somehow.

Harald kissed her neck possessively and whispered in her ear, "Just wait till I get you home. . . ."

Home. The word chilled Faith. Of course he would take her home—and then how would she get rid of him, short of World War III? Faith saw the ugly confrontation bearing down on her with the force of an avalanche. She remembered, sickeningly, that they had never had an argument that Harald hadn't won.

That thought ruined the rest of the party for Faith. She circulated politely and talked and smiled, all the time with her mind jumping ahead to the inevitable clash awaiting her. If only Harald would listen to reason.

A familiar melody wafted across the dance floor, infiltrating Faith's consciousness like a potent drug. "Some Enchanted Evening." With a pang, Faith recalled the last time she'd heard the song: she'd been in Ken Powell's arms at the Plaza, and Nick Justin had watched them together and thought they were lovers.

Nick watched her now. Faith suddenly felt his scrutiny too painful to bear and left the room by the closest door.

She walked out into the night, among the bright trees that even in summer were strung with festive miniature lights. She wasn't surprised when Nick followed her; it even felt natural when, without a word, he took her in his arms and glided her gently across the brick path, beneath the leafy branches.

"I've wanted to do this," he muttered over the faint strains of the music, "ever since that night at the Plaza—"

"Don't talk about that night," she said in an urgent whisper. "Don't talk at all."

He obeyed. Faith closed her eyes and rested her cheek against the soft lapel of his jacket. Her breasts were crushed against him so tightly she could scarcely breathe, but Faith didn't mind. If this could just go on forever, she thought, and I'd never have to face Prue and Harald. . . .

When the music ended Nick took Faith's hand and led her across the road into the park. Faith followed without question. She didn't stop to think about the implications, didn't care. Every nerve in her body tingled with anticipation.

Nick stopped beside a bench half-hidden by blooming lilacs. He looked down at Faith. His face was shuttered, hostile.

Faith's knees grew weak. What if Nick didn't feel for her what she felt for him? She had so little experience—

he could toy with her and she wouldn't know the difference. Faith collapsed onto the bench, hesitant, unwilling to make the first move and perhaps be rebuffed, although she was certain she would do something outrageous if he didn't kiss her soon.

Nick spoke harshly. "We have business to settle."

"Business?" The cold word, and the cold voice behind it froze Faith's soul.

"Police business. You gave me your word, if you recall—"

"Of course." Her voice shook, and she fought to keep it level. "I'll keep my promise. I'll go to the police about the robbery tomorrow."

"Make sure you do." Nick pulled a card from his wallet. He wrote a few words on the back of the card and handed it to Faith. "That's the case number, the precinct and the arresting officer's name. There's my home number and my office number, if you need me. I'll call the precinct and tell them to expect you."

"Fine," Faith said numbly.

"One more thing." The words rapped out in staccato delivery of the professional newscaster. "You have until ten o'clock Monday morning. If you haven't made a statement by then, I'll stop by the Foundation and escort you to the precinct personally. And tell everyone just how the incident happened, background and all."

"That's blackmail," Faith said clearly.

"You're hardly in a position to protest," he reminded her. "Ten o'clock Monday morning."

Surely he couldn't be walking away? Faith rose from the bench in dismay.

"Wait—"

"What is it?"

His harsh manner puzzled Faith. It was as if he suddenly hated her. Why? What had she done? With nervous hands she pleated the silk of her skirt. "Then you—you haven't said anything about my book?" she asked.

"Not yet. I guess you deserve some time to get your affairs in order."

"But what about your story?" she ventured, knowing she was treading on dangerous ground. "Will you kill it?"

His brows drew together. "No."

"Not even if I go to the police?"

"Not for any reason."

Faith was aghast. "But you'll ruin my life! How could you be such a monster as to put the Fanny Duvall story on the air?"

"Fanny Duvall is newsworthy," Nick said calmly. "It's not my fault that she's also Faith Daniels. And let me remind you that none of this would have happened if you hadn't gone to that damn awards dinner."

"So what?"

"So it's your fault, Fanny. Face it," Nick said impatiently. "Nobody held a gun to your head and forced you to go. You went because you wanted to and now you have to pay the price."

"I didn't know the price would be so high," Faith said, her voice soft as a child's. She discovered, to her horror, that tears were rising in her eyes.

"That's a lot of passion to waste on Harald Clinton, your aunt and a job you can't stand," Nick mocked her and Faith's spine stiffened.

"I doubt you'll understand this," she snapped, "but they're all I have."

"Oh, wouldn't I?" His hands turned her around to face him, not gently. Nick looked at her, his face hard and unyielding. A shock of dark hair fell over his forehead as he bent his head to hers.

Nick kissed her, his lips hard and violent against hers. This was not the feather-soft, teasing kiss of earlier in the evening, but something rough and untamed unleashed in him. It thrilled Faith, and she parted her lips, willing him to possess her mouth; she was totally unprepared for the force with which he did.

"Nick—"

Her words vanished into a cry as he pulled her down on the bench. Nick drew her body against his and kissed her even more deeply, his passion igniting a fierceness inside Faith. With a wild wonder she found herself kissing him back, cradling Nick's head between her hands, pressing her body to his in open desire. Faith had never responded to a man this way, but her momentary shame was no match for the delight of Nick's touch.

Let him think what he liked of her, she decided. What did it matter if he knew how much she wanted him? She could feel how much he wanted her.

Nick pulled away and stared down at her intently, as if trying to read her deepest thoughts. Faith knew her emotions were written all over her face, but she didn't try to mask them. She shivered openly as Nick stroked her hair, her cheek, her throat. He ran his fingers over her bare shoulder and down to her breast.

Faith stopped breathing.

For a moment they hung in limbo, neither moving, then Faith moaned with pleasure and pulled Nick down on top of her, kissing him with a passion she hadn't guessed she possessed.

She reveled in the feeling of his weight upon her, loved hearing him groan with mingled pleasure and desire. Loved the sense that, for once in his life, even Nick Justin was out of control—

Then, suddenly, Nick wrenched himself away. He rose and stood over her, his chest heaving with the effort it cost him to breathe. He stared at Faith as if carving her image in his memory.

Faith's arms were flung wide, her lips parted and

glistening, her nipples standing out clearly beneath the pink silk. Her desire—more, her consent—shone out of her eyes.

But if she thought she would melt him, bring him back to her arms, she was mistaken. Nick's voice was as harsh as a curse.

"Monday morning," he said. "Remember." And he disappeared through the parking lot.

Faith's body trembled, her head spun, her heart ached. Nick had wanted her, wanted her completely; inexperienced as she was, she knew *that*. His searing mouth, his ragged breathing, his taut and hardened body all gave evidence of his desire for her. What was wrong, then? Did Nick still not trust her? Did he, perhaps, think Faith was using him, that she would stop at nothing to keep her story from the public?

When Faith at last sat up, she found the card he'd given her lying on the ground beneath her heel. She rescued the card and turned it over and over in her hand. Unreal. Nothing was real but the memory of Nick's kisses, of his wanting her. Pleasure still surged through her at the memory.

Faith rose dreamily and turned to walk back to the Tavern on the Green. She had, after all, responsibilities to attend to.

"And miles to go before I sleep," she quoted drowsily. Then she saw something that brought her fully awake.

Someone stood across the road, watching her. A man. Harald.

6

Oh, no!"

The words slipped from Faith's throat, a whispered prayer, no more. How long had Harald stood in the shadows across the road, watching her?

Had he seen her in Nick's arms?

Faith forced herself to walk toward the shadowy figure, a false gay smile plastered on her face. Act natural, she told herself. Assume he's seen nothing.

She greeted Harald with an expectant smile. "I didn't realize it was so late—"

"The hell you didn't." His hand shot out and encircled her wrist. He pushed her toward the restaurant entrance. "Get your things. We're going home. Now."

Faith murmured an assent, but her heart sank. There was no point in argument. Harald had seen enough to make him angry; now she could only try to avoid an explosion.

While they passed through the dining room and shook

the hands of countless acquaintances, Faith worried, but she couldn't think of any way to make amends.

Harald's cold silence as he escorted her home grew more and more threatening. The blocks passed by quickly as Faith hurried to keep up with his long strides. When she meekly asked him to slow down his speed increased.

Oh, help, she thought, he's furious. At least Bonnie would be there when they got to the apartment. He couldn't kill her in front of a witness.

Faith's hand shook as she fitted her key into the lock. Harald's hand came over hers and twisted the key in a savage, impatient motion. The heavy door swung open onto the dark stairway.

Faith shivered as she slowly mounted the stairs. For once, she would have been glad of Prue's nosy presence in the lower duplex of the family brownstone. She imagined Prue's door sliding open an inch behind its chain bolt, Prue's hard blue eyes peering out. But, tonight, Prue was not there to protect Faith; she would be the last to leave the Tavern on the Green.

Faith unlocked the door to her apartment and walked inside. The living room was pitch-black.

"Bonnie?" she called, alarmed.

Faith clicked on the light. No sign of her roommate. She checked the bedrooms, the bath. No one.

"We're alone," Harald said, his voice eerie. "And high time. I want to talk to you."

He snapped the lock on the door. Then he flung his jacket across the back of a chair and began to walk toward Faith.

"Harald! You don't have to look so menacing!" Faith tried to sound teasing but only managed to sound nervous. "Sit down and we'll talk—"

"Talk!" Harald exploded, and added several expletives. "That isn't what you were interested in when I saw you in the park."

"I—I can explain," Faith began, without the faintest idea of what she could say.

"Tell me I was seeing things. Tell me that wasn't you with Nick Justin, carrying on like a ten-dollar hooker."

Faith started to say it was nothing, but the lie stuck in her throat. She realized that the few moments she'd spent with Nick meant more to her than months with Harald.

"Well?" Harald demanded. He grabbed Faith by the shoulder and pulled her around to face him. "Aren't you going to say anything? I think you'd agree some explanation is due, baby."

Baby. The word rankled, kicked up an anger inside Faith that smothered her fear. "Oh, you're due an explanation, all right, darling," she said, and stressed the last word with a sickeningly sweet inflection. "Maybe you'd better sit down."

"I'll stand."

"Fine." Faith drew a deep breath and then, although her knees were shaking, she summoned her calmest voice and told Harald she was breaking their engagement.

At first Harald said nothing at all, just looked at her with a face devoid of expression. "What did you say?"

Faith repeated her statement and watched his handsome face turn surprised, then sullen and finally angry.

"You can't be serious," he blurted. "You're out of your mind."

"Possibly," Faith agreed. "But I'm sure we're not right for each other. I'm sorry," she added softly as she pulled the heavy diamond from her finger and dropped the ring into Harald's hand. "Truly. The mistake was all mine. I should never have said yes in the first place."

"I don't believe this," Harald muttered, as he paced back and forth in front of the fireplace. "You don't want to marry me?"

"No. I don't," she repeated patiently.

"Why?"

Faith had to stifle a laugh. It was plain that Harald couldn't think of a single reason, short of insanity. Faith offered some bromide about them not being suited for each other, about not having known her own mind. Harald cut her off in midsentence.

"Damn you!" His face twisted into ugliness as he flung the ring to the carpet. "Don't give me that 'I was too young and innocent' routine. Admit the truth. It's some other guy, isn't it?"

As Faith grew pale, Harald's voice rose in anger. "Now I see! You've been having an affair!"

"No," Faith protested, stung.

"No, hell." Harald spat out the words. "There's always been another guy, hasn't there? But he wouldn't come across with marriage, so you thought you'd string me along—"

"Harald, calling off our marriage is just common sense," Faith insisted. "You and me, we just don't belong together. This has nothing to do with any other man." But against her will her mind filled with an image of Nick.

"Justin!" Harald cried, and Faith knew her face gave her away. Harald smacked the fireplace mantel so violently that Faith jumped.

"What a fool I've been." Harald swore. "After I saw you two together—how long have you been sleeping with him?"

"I've never slept with him," Faith said, with great dignity and equal precision.

"Bull," Harald said, and lunged at Faith so that she skipped backwards. For a moment they stared at each other as violence crackled in the air between them. Faith clutched her throat automatically in self-protection; she was sure Harald intended to strangle her. When, a few seconds later, his tense hands dropped to his sides, she knew the impulse had been there.

"You're a fool," Harald said bitterly.

"Probably," Faith agreed. They both looked down at the diamond on the rug and for a moment Faith felt sorry for Harald. He sat down numbly on the couch, obviously trying to salvage what he could from the situation.

"You know," he said at last, "Nick Justin will never offer you what I can. You could never be anything more to him than a one-night stand."

"Thanks a lot," Faith muttered. "It's wonderful to know how highly you value me."

"Face facts," Harald snarled. "I didn't think even you could be so immature that you'd sacrifice your whole future to some fling."

"Nick Justin has nothing whatever to do with what's wrong between us," Faith insisted. "You and I could never be happy together. You must see that now."

"What I see is that you're being a damned stubborn fool. But I won't hold it against you—"

"Big of you," Faith said sarcastically.

"Seriously, baby," Harald said earnestly. "You can't call off the wedding. Plans have been made, the invitations are printed, the St. Regis is booked, even the campaign schedule has been juggled—"

"Oh, blast the campaign schedule. That always came first with you, didn't it?"

"So what?" Harald shrugged. "That's reality. That's my career, remember?"

"Then you'll be glad to find all that extra time on your schedule," Faith retorted. "I'm sure you'll put it to good use."

"You'll change your mind before then," was his confident prediction.

"I'm afraid not."

"We'll see." Harald smiled smugly. "I give you about three days before you're crying on my doorstep."

Faith seethed with frustration. "Don't hold your breath," she retorted, and Harald laughed.

"Don't worry, I won't cancel the arrangements in the meantime. But I will have to tell Prue about your—shall we call it momentary change of heart?"

He paused to let Faith absorb the veiled threat. "She won't be pleased."

"Tough," Faith said angrily. "She'll just have to struggle along."

"What the hell's gotten into you?" Harald demanded. "Why, Prue and the Foundation are your whole life—"

"Not anymore," Faith declared resolutely. "In fact, I'm thinking of leaving the Foundation." She was astonished to hear the words coming from her mouth, and more astonished to realize that she meant them.

"What?" Harald was flabbergasted. "Leave the Foundation? And do what, may I ask? Crochet?"

"Write," Faith replied.

"Write? You mean, for a living?" Harald laughed aloud, and Faith felt as if he'd poured acid into her soul. "You'll never make it, baby. You won't last six months."

"That's what you think," Faith snapped. "I'm not a novice, Harald. I've already published one novel—"

"Oh, sure, and that's why we've all heard so much about it, haven't we?" Harald mocked. "Really, Faith. Stop bluffing. You've got no talent for it."

"Bluffing!" Faith sputtered in fury, unable to find words to express her anger. "Harald, I think you'd better leave."

"Fine," he said, still sounding amused. "You've got my phone number. When you're ready to apologize, give me a call. I'll probably forgive you." He picked up his jacket from the back of a chair. "Just don't wait too long."

"You can wait until hell freezes over," Faith muttered, and locked the door behind him.

By morning the night's events seemed cloaked in an aura of unreality. Faith moved briskly through her morning routine with a cool detachment she recognized as a form of shock. After last night's fireworks, even her obligatory visit to the police station seemed tame by comparison.

The interrogation and the filing of the complaint were not nearly so uncomfortable as Faith had feared. However, Faith suspected that Sergeant McCall's friendly attitude was due largely to Nick Justin's words on her behalf. That Nick had prepared her way was evident but that didn't stop Faith from wondering what Nick would have done if she hadn't kept her promise to him.

"I'm sure he'd have gone to Aunt Prue," she said to Bonnie later, "and had me hauled off in disgrace, just like he threatened."

"Really?" Bonnie commented. "Would he have brought cameras? I'd've loved to see that on TV."

"Bite your tongue," Faith said. "It's going to be bad enough as it is, trying to tell Aunt Prue I wrote *Blood Poisoning*. Much less that I want to leave the Foundation to do more of the same." She sighed. "I'm still trying to find a tactful way to break the news," she added grimly. "You can imagine how Nick Justin would tell her."

"Flat out," Bonnie said. "Not necessarily the worst way to handle it, either."

"I don't want Prue to have a heart attack," Faith objected.

"Fair enough," Bonnie said, and then asked in a deceptively casual voice, "When are you seeing Nick Justin again?"

"Never," Faith said emphatically. Bonnie gave her a skeptical look. "Oh, no, not you, too. Why doesn't anybody believe me when I say there's nothing between us?"

"Maybe because I saw you two dancing. Whew!"

"Oh, that." Faith shrugged. "Doesn't mean a thing. That's just a reporter in pursuit of a story. That's all I am, as far as Nick Justin is concerned—news on the hoof. The lust is all on my side."

"Don't be too sure," Bonnie cautioned. "I've seen the way he looks at you."

"Like a slide under a microscope," Faith groaned. "Just research."

Bonnie rose. "He's bound and determined to put the Fanny Duvall story on the air, huh? Whether you want him to or not?"

"Neither rain, nor snow, nor sleet—"

"You can't find some way to persuade him to kill the story?"

"Nope," Faith said. "He's immune to all feminine wiles."

"He didn't look immune to me," Bonnie remarked. "He looked hot as a firecracker."

"He always looks that way. It's his nature."

"Wow," said Bonnie. "Lucky you."

Faith picked up one of the sofa pillows and threw it at her roommate. Bonnie ducked, laughing, and reached for the ringing phone.

"It's for you. Aunt Prue."

Faith grimaced. "Three guesses what this is about."

Ten minutes later Faith slammed the phone down.

"I guess Harald had a little talk with her," Bonnie said mildly.

"Oh, he told her everything," Faith responded angrily, "and now she wants to come up and straighten me out."

"What's she planning to do—drag you to the church in chains?"

"Don't laugh," Faith said. "Although I think her tactics will be a bit more subtle than that. More like the Chinese water torture."

Bonnie looked nervously toward the door. "In that case, why don't we leave? How about some coffee and a danish down at the French bakery?"

"How about six hundred extra calories?" Faith teased. "Actually, I was thinking of hiding out with a good book. Say, a nice, bloodcurdling mystery."

In the end Bonnie agreed, and to the bookstore they went. Faith selected two mysteries, a collection of humorous essays, a historical romance and a paperback that promised to teach her to assert herself in three easy lessons.

Faith eventually tracked Bonnie down in the reference section, her curly head buried in a large red volume. "It says here he was born in Akron, Ohio. Akron! Can you believe it?" Bonnie had the provincialism of most native New Yorkers: she felt anyone born outside the five boroughs started life with an immense handicap.

"What are you reading, for heaven's sake?" Faith turned the book to its binding: *Who's Who in America.* "Nick Justin?"

"Mm-hmm. Did you know he started out on a newspaper when he was sixteen?" Bonnie asked.

"No."

"And he wrote for the *Times* when he was at Columbia. Got into broadcast work after that, at a little station in Florida."

Faith peered at the listing. Nick's rapid rise from local newsman to network correspondent to star of *Newsview* was all there in stark print: places, dates, awards.

"Ah, here's the good stuff. Personal." Bonnie winked knowingly. "Married Cynthia Damon, sculptor—good grief, he was only twenty-two then! One child, Rebecca.

She's about six, I guess. Divorced two years ago."
Bonnie closed the book and gave Faith a broad smile.
"Sounds to me like an ideal candidate for matrimony."

"Hah!" Faith snorted. "You'd better not take up
fortune-telling as a career, girl—you'd starve." Faith
didn't admit that she herself had done some investigation
while rummaging among the books. She'd found a
volume on Cynthia Justin's work in the art section. Faith
was impressed by Cynthia's talent, although she pre-
ferred the early bronze figures to the later abstract
shapes. However, Faith had found the photographs of
Nick's ex-wife herself quite disconcerting.

Cynthia Justin had been a petite, raven-haired beauty,
with a voluptuous figure and an air of smoldering sensuality. Faith thought regretfully of her own still boyishly
slender figure and her Madonna-like face, and sighed at
her own foolishness. She had cherished a secret hope
that Nick would call her, now that he knew her identity.
Fat chance, she thought now, recalling Cynthia, you're
simply not his type.

Faith got through her disappointment by burying
herself in her writing. Even on Saturday morning the
following week, she was on her favorite bench at the
gazebo by seven-thirty.

As she worked, the day grew hotter and the park more
crowded. The pond in front of her was dotted with
boats—first one solitary rower, then two boats, then a
cluster. By noon there were dozens of rowboats plying
the pond, their red and green and grey hulls gliding
across the still surface.

Faith loved the water. Some days she would take a
boat out herself, row it down to the north end of the
pond, and just rest on her oars. As the boat drifted, Faith
would contemplate her problems, and often the solution
would come to her.

Faith looked up from her work, frustrated. The scene she was writing was a difficult one, a confrontation between the heroine and the man she was destined to love. Not only that, but the man sounded disconcertingly like Nick Justin.

Damn. A boat came in to the pier at her feet; a young man with sandy hair and a wide grin invited her to join him.

"No, but thanks!" she called. He smiled and rowed away, but Faith's concentration was broken. She lost herself in a fantasy: the boat which stopped alongside the gazebo had a dark-haired man at the oars, a man whose hazel eyes could glow green with passion. . . .

Faith gave up her attempt to discipline her wayward thoughts and called Figaro to her side. She petted him affectionately, then threw her pad and pens into her shoulder bag, dusted off her jeans, and headed downtown.

Faith strolled at a casual pace, waiting for some vista to strike her fancy. Only the baseball field beckoned to her. Here children and adults played side by side, and the crack of bats and shouts of hope filled the summer air. Faith stopped to watch the end of a game and Figaro spotted a crowd of children playing with a Frisbee and loped over to join them.

Faith's eyes followed him wistfully. Oh, to be that innocent again, she thought as she watched the children. She had never known that lighthearted aspect of childhood. From the day of her father's death, Faith had been a miniature adult, burdened with unpleasant realities and an unsympathetic guardian.

If I ever have children, she thought fiercely, I'll see that they laugh and play all they can, while they can.

Faith noticed a little girl slowly approach Figaro; something about her reminded Faith that at that age she'd been alone, too. She walked over. "Hi."

"Hi." The girl's manner was friendly but hesitant, as if she thought Faith might take the dog away. "Is he yours?"

"Yep. His name's Figaro."

"He's a great dog," the child volunteered, her wide green eyes earnest.

"Thanks, I think so too. Do you have a dog?"

Faith helped the conversation along, and observed her small companion curiously. The girl was tall for her age, slender but sturdily built in her no-nonsense denim jeans and a red-and-white striped top. Her manner was equally direct, full of unguarded enthusiasm and a candor that could make Faith bubble with laughter. She had straight chestnut hair, cut short, and the energy of the born tomboy.

Faith could hardly imagine a girl more different from the shy, dreamy, withdrawn little blonde she had been, yet there were similarities that distressed her. The sudden shadow in the eyes, the too-adult speech, the sense of grownup burdens on the square little shoulders.

"I don't want to keep you from your friends," Faith said finally, reluctant to leave her.

"It's okay," the child chirped. "I don't know anybody here. Except my dad. He's playing baseball. I'm going to watch the game."

"Oh."

"Would you like to come? The team's pretty good," she added, as if that might be some incentive.

Faith read the unspoken appeal in the girl's eyes. "Sure," Faith said instantly, with an enthusiasm she had never previously felt for baseball. "That sounds like fun."

"Great." The little face lit in a smile that split the lower half of her face into a beaming triangle. There was something familiar about her smile, Faith thought. Come to think of it, wasn't there something familiar about the set of her shoulders, the uptilted chin, the green eyes?

Oh, brother, Faith told herself disgustedly, you're in worse shape than you thought if you're seeing Nick Justin all over the place. She negotiated her way into the bleachers that overlooked the baseball diamond.

And then she saw him. For a wild moment Faith feared she was hallucinating. Nick Justin! Not reflected in the child's face, but standing on the field. He wore a red T-shirt with his network's logo emblazoned on the front.

Faith's heart sank down to her knees. She wanted to bolt, yet perversity held her right where she was. She had every right to watch this game; it was a public field. And there was something mesmerizing about watching Nick play.

Slowly Faith realized that her little companion had talked nonstop, had pointed out each player on the red-shirted team and called each by name.

"Oh, by the way, I'm Becky."

"Pleased to meet you," she said gravely. "I'm Faith." Becky. Rebecca. Of course the girl was a Justin—Faith could see it simply in the way she lifted her head and looked out at the world, her gaze direct and steady, her green eyes alive with curiosity.

"Faith. That's a funny name. What do people call you?"

"Faith, I'm afraid." No one had ever called Faith by a pet name. Except for a man who called her Fanny.

To her surprise, Faith enjoyed the game. Becky proved to be a fountain of information about such mysteries as sacrifice flies and the hit-and-run. And Nick was an excellent athlete. Faith let herself get caught up in the game but determined that, when the game ended, she would leave before Nick could notice her.

She was afraid to see him face to face, or to speak— memories of their last meeting swirled in her mind and she felt vulnerable.

But she had reckoned without Figaro, who balked at

leaving his new companion. As Faith struggled to attach his leash, she heard her name called in a piping voice and looked up to see Becky hailing Nick. He was in the process of stripping off his T-shirt to change to a fresh sport shirt, and the sight of his naked torso held Faith immobile for a fatal second.

Nick glanced up, saw her, froze: he looked Faith up and down as if he couldn't quite decide whether he were blessed or cursed.

Faith slowly vaulted down from the bleachers, her face flaming.

"Hello, Fanny," Nick said at last.

"Daddy! Her name's Faith!"

"Hello, Nick." Faith's fingers tightened convulsively on Figaro's leash. "Good game. You play very well." Lord, how inane, she thought. As if he cares.

"Thanks." Oddly enough, Nick seemed to find the moment difficult, too. "Um—thanks for keeping an eye on Becky. I appreciate it."

"It was a pleasure," Faith said honestly.

"She needed me to keep an eye on her!" Becky interjected. "Dad, she doesn't know a thing about baseball!"

"Oh, no. What an ordeal for you." Nick's voice was all sympathy, and Faith warmed to it. "I'm sorry if you got roped into staying—"

"Not at all," she demurred. "I enjoyed myself."

"Well, at least let me buy you lunch to make amends." As Faith hesitated, he added, "I'm starving. Aren't you?"

"I could eat a horse," Becky announced.

"Then let's round up some hot dogs and sodas and have a picnic on the grass. How's that?" Nick put his arm around his daughter and Becky giggled with approval. "Fanny?"

"Oh, I should be going," she said, embarrassed. She

had no right to intrude on Nick's time with Becky; they probably had little enough time to spend together. . . .

Becky protested, immediately and vocally. Nick shushed her. "Miss Daniels may have other things to do, Becky. It's not fair to put pressure on her—"

"I don't want to be in the way," Faith mumbled.

"You're not in the way! Please?"

Faith looked at the pleading face, remembered that the child had only recently lost her mother, and the list of afternoon chores went straight out of Faith's head.

"You know what? I'd love to have lunch."

Nick shot Faith a grateful glance and she felt suddenly warm all over.

"Oh, goody," said Becky. "Can I walk Figaro?"

Faith meekly handed over the leash. The younger Justin, she thought ruefully, showed signs of being as irresistible as the elder. Becky skipped ahead down the path, leaving Nick to fall in at Faith's side.

"Thank you for that," he said quietly. "Becky hasn't had much female companionship lately. It means a lot to her."

"I enjoyed myself," Faith told him again.

"Still, I'm sorry if Becky pressured you. She can be quite a steamroller when there's something she wants—"

"Can't imagine where she gets that," Faith commented dryly.

Nick laughed. "You have a point." He added, "She's only been living in the city a short time, and she doesn't have many friends here yet."

"I understand. I know all about what it's like to be a lonely little girl."

"I guess you would," Nick responded, after a moment's thought. "You were pretty young when your father died—"

"I was five."

Nick watched her intently, as if unsure how to phrase his next question. "You didn't . . . see it, I hope?"

"No. It was a car bomb, you know, and Mummy and I were blocks away at the time. But I did see what was left of the car . . . afterwards." She knew Nick could see the pain in her eyes before she looked away. "Believe me, that was enough."

There was a silence, at last broken by Nick's rueful voice. "You know, I keep remembering what I said the night I met you. At the MWA banquet. How I harangued you about the violence in your work. I think I said some fool thing about not understanding why a pretty little blonde would be obsessed with murder—"

"Forget it," Faith said abruptly. "You had no way of knowing what my life had been—"

"I was out of line, so let me apologize," he said firmly. "I should learn not to make assumptions like that."

"Old habits die hard."

"Yeah, I guess so," he said softly. "But I understand a lot more now."

"About my work?"

"Yeah. And about you. About the contradictions."

Faith didn't want to get into a discussion of her "contradictions," or in fact anything about her personal life. She smoothly turned the conversation back to Nick. "And I understand a lot more about you," she said swiftly, "now that I've met Becky."

"I appreciate the time you're spending with her," he replied soberly. "She's had it tough lately. Her mother—" He stopped and swallowed hard.

"I know you were divorced. I suppose it was hard for you to see Becky, after?"

"Damn near impossible. Cynthia had a studio in the Catskills, and I got up there every weekend I could, but I never saw Cynthia if I could help it. I'd just collect Becky and leave." He hesitated, a bit embarrassed. "I know that sounds callous, but we fought terribly if we were together, and I couldn't see the point of exposing Becky to more of that."

"Of course not," Faith said sympathetically.

"But that's why I didn't know." Nick paused, and at Faith's puzzled look, he explained, "How much Cynthia had been drinking. Not until it was too late. I keep thinking there must have been something I could have done. . . ."

"It wasn't your fault." Moved by his distress, Faith put a comforting hand on Nick's arm. "If she wouldn't help herself, there's nothing you could have done." Faith remembered her own mother, wasting away in an upstairs room among her husband's pictures, dying of a broken heart. Cecily Daniels hadn't drunk herself to death, but she had fled from life's pressures as surely as had Cynthia Justin.

"At least I could have gotten Becky out of there," Nick muttered.

"And broken the law? Cynthia had custody."

"To hell with the law," Nick said hoarsely. "I'm just starting to learn what it was like up there. Becky never complained. Never said a word."

"She must have loved her mother."

"Yeah. A damn sight more than her mother ever loved her." Nick looked away, as if the admission cost him pain. "Cynthia didn't want children. Never did."

"But surely, Becky—" Faith stopped and blushed. How had the conversation gotten this personal?

"Becky was an accident." Nick's long fingers fretted with the leather lacing on his baseball glove. "Cynthia wanted an abortion, but I just couldn't . . . I put a lot of pressure on her to have the baby. Gave her an ultimatum. Some nerve, huh?"

Faith said nothing.

"I was sure," he went on, "that once she saw the baby

her feelings would change, that she'd love our child." He groaned. "Some of our friends tried to warn me that life wasn't that simple and black-and-white, but I was just too headstrong to listen." He looked at Faith, abashed. "You get the picture."

"But I'm sure she loved Becky," Faith protested. "Who wouldn't?"

"Oh, she loved Becky—but she hated parenting. Hated what it did to her life."

"Then why didn't she give you custody? Since you were the one who wanted a child in the first place?"

"That's just it," Nick growled. "Cynthia knew how I wanted Becky, so she kept her to punish me. Unfortunately, it's Becky who's suffered the most."

His hand exploded against the pocket of the glove; the mitt popped and Faith jumped.

"I wonder if I can ever make it up to her."

"You already have," Faith said comfortingly. "Becky adores you. Don't you know that?"

"If she only knew how much I'm to blame for what she's been through."

"She knows how much you love her. That's all that matters." Faith's voice was earnest. "Believe me. I know."

"You're quite a comfort," Nick said, and took her hand.

They walked in silence for a few minutes, Faith intensely conscious of Nick's hand against hers. They watched Becky and Figaro romp and run, often veering off the path to chase squirrels over grass and around trees.

"That's quite a tomboy you've got there." Faith grinned.

"I know." Nick sounded amused, but a hint of worry showed between his brows. "I think she needs more of a woman's touch."

"What, Mary Janes and frilly dresses?" Faith snorted.

"You let her run and climb trees all she wants. I wish someone had done that for me when I was her age. Maybe I wouldn't be such a scaredy-cat now."

"You mean to tell me you've never climbed a tree?"

"Never."

"You're kidding."

"I'm scared of heights," Faith said defensively.

"That's not high." Nick pointed to a huge chestnut tree dead in their path. The tree forked a mere seven feet off the ground.

Faith shook her head. "No way. When they install escalators, then I'll climb trees."

"It's never too late to learn." A wicked grin began to spread across Nick's face.

"Oh, no you don't." She guessed his intention and ran ahead; he caught her by the belt of her jeans and tugged her backwards.

"Nick, I can't!" Faith was frantic. "I told you, I'm scared of heights. Besides, my shoes—"

"Just take them off," he said, and proceeded to unbuckle her sandals.

"You're mad!" she protested as she felt whatever control she had in the situation slipping away.

"Come on, you just said it was something you always wanted to do. You'll never get a better chance." His voice was seductive. "I'll be right behind you—"

"You are such a bully, Nick Justin," Faith fumed, but a crowd was gathering around them, and she didn't want to wind up on page four of the *New York Post*. Before she quite knew what was happening, Faith was halfway up the craggy bark. She blocked out everything but Nick's instructions: placed her hands where he told her, moved her body ever so slowly upward. Her heart raced with fear. Don't think, Faith told herself, just move; she felt the nearness of Nick's body beneath her and it propelled her upward.

Becky shouted encouragement. Figaro barked. An ever-increasing crowd of New Yorkers—Faith remembered, too late, that New Yorkers would watch anything —gathered at the base of the tree.

One foot up. Another. Her hands and feet were scratched and sore. Faith finally maneuvered herself to a sitting position, wrapped her arms around two branches, and clung so tightly she nearly stopped the circulation in her arms. She didn't feel safe—not at all—she felt horrendously dizzy. Nick pulled himself up beside her and laughed.

"You heartless bully," she hissed. "See what you've got me into?"

"It's not so bad," he said. "I knew you could do it if you tried."

"Easy for you to say. I'm shaking like a leaf." Faith offered a trembling wrist as evidence.

"But look around you. It's beautiful."

Faith had to admit the view was spectacular. Ahead of her was the skyline of Fifty-ninth Street poking through the green of the leaves. She smiled and looked across to where Nick had wedged himself against the branches, the muscles rippling across his shoulders and arms. He looked devilishly attractive.

"That's better," he said softly, and Faith realized that her expression had changed as she looked at him. She quickly rearranged her features.

"Dad, I'm hungry!" Becky called. "Are you going to stay up there all day?"

He laughed. "No." Nick vaulted to the ground gracefully, then reached up for Faith. "Come on down."

Panic engulfed her. She couldn't move. Faith tried to follow Nick's instructions, to turn herself around. Her sweaty palms slipped on the bark and she lurched as she tried to find a handhold, then slid disastrously. Faith clung to the branch and tried to lock her legs around the trunk. Her feet slipped, pulling her down.

"Fanny!" Nick's voice shattered the mist in her brain. "Listen!"

She tried to do what he said, but couldn't. Her limbs were made of rubber. She felt her hands slip.

"Fanny!" Nick's voice penetrated again. "Jump!"

Faith risked another glance down and saw Nick standing directly below her, his arms held out to catch her.

He couldn't, of course. She would thud against the ground, or her weight would carry him down with her. But Faith's palms were soaked with sweat and she couldn't hold on any longer. She had no choice.

She closed her eyes and jumped.

7

Moments later she felt Nick's arms close round her; she was caught and held. How strong he is! she thought.

For a moment she clung to Nick, content to feel the power in his arms, to inhale the musky scent of his skin. Funny, the sudden dependence didn't frighten her—she just smiled up at Nick rather dreamily and watched the dimple flash at the left corner of his mouth.

"Aw-right!" yelled one of the men standing around the base of the tree. Applause and laughter broke out. Faith had forgotten her audience; now, shy, she stirred and Nick set her on her feet.

"No harm done?" he asked.

"No harm done," Faith assured him, "if I can just find my shoes."

Nick handed her sandals to her and she sat and tugged them on before he could offer assistance. She'd better be wary of too much physical contact with Mr. Justin, she decided. Her heart still raced from the moment she'd spent in his arms.

Faith determined to be casual through lunch. She focused her attention on Becky rather than Nick, and was surprised to see how much that pleased him. And when, after a long and laughing meal, they played tag along the bank of the rowing pond, Faith saw for the first time a loving, gentle side to the formidable dragon of television news. Nick's concern for his daughter, his sensitivity to her needs, was a revelation that struck Faith into silence and private, uncomfortable speculation. Surely a man capable of such wholehearted love for his daughter had much to offer in other capacities—

Faith was so lost in thought that she didn't notice Nick's approach until he spoke.

"A penny for your thoughts," he murmured, as he collapsed on the ground beside her.

"Actually, I was thinking of what a good father you are," Faith said, censoring the second part of her thought. "You seem to sense just what Becky needs."

He flushed and looked at his hands, as if her praise made him uncomfortable. Well, that's a change, Faith thought, I've embarrassed him.

"You love children, don't you?" he asked suddenly.

"Very much. Maybe that's funny, because I've never been around kids much," Faith admitted. "Then again, maybe it's 'cause I was so lonely when I was little that now, nothing makes me happier than to be surrounded by kids."

"I'm surprised you don't have a bunch of your own," Nick observed, not entirely innocently.

"I can't do it by myself," Faith responded absently. Then she caught the twinkle in Nick's eye, considered the implications, and blushed.

"You keep looking out at the boats," he commented, changing the subject. "Would you like to go rowing?"

Damn. She'd forgotten his acute powers of observation. Faith began a polite denial but Nick stopped her. "I'd love to," she finally confessed, "but this is not the day for it. With Figaro and Becky—"

"No problem," he said. "Trust me." Ten minutes later they were out on the pond, gliding across the glassy surface.

Faith insisted on taking an oar, so she and Nick sat side by side on one of the hot wooden plank benches. Becky sat opposite, one hand trailing in the water, the other hand restraining Figaro from jumping overboard in his enthusiasm. At first the boat went mostly in circles, then Faith learned to time her stroke with Nick's so they went smoothly across the water.

They talked about the pond and the park—Nick, not at all to Faith's surprise, turned out to be an expert on Central Park lore—and when Faith mentioned her habit of writing at the gazebo, Nick turned the conversation to Faith's work. When half an hour had passed Faith's mind was so teeming with fresh ideas that she apologized, pulled her notebook from her shoulder bag, and scribbled down several notes.

"So I won't forget. This is great stuff," she explained.

Nick laughed—a laugh of pleasure, not condescension. He rested on the oars and let the boat drift beneath the willows at the lake's edge, and told Faith to take all the time she needed.

Faith fleetingly considered what Harald would have said if she'd ever ignored him to pull out her notebook and scribble away. She shuddered.

Only later, when Faith went back to those rushed pages, did she realize how Nick's questions had opened floodgates in her mind. Her respect for him increased as she realized how he had helped her, without his own personality intruding into her work.

When Faith finished, Becky insisted on exploring the gazebo. Nick rowed obediently in to the dock. Faith pointed out her favorite bench; Becky scrambled out of the boat and inspected it as if it were King Tut's tomb.

"So you wrote a book, right here," she said, awed.

"Right there," Faith answered cheerfully. "And that's where you'll find me every morning. It's my favorite place in the whole park."

"My favorite place is the carousel." Becky clambered back into the boat. "Where's your favorite place, Daddy?"

"Right here with you," Nick said smoothly, but his eyes met Faith's and she went crimson. Nick lifted an oar and rowed. Faith sat as if rooted, unable to flirt back or frame a reply.

"Are you going to row, or not?" Nick demanded. He dipped his oar and splashed water at her.

"Tote that barge, lift that bale," Faith grumbled. The tension broke and they rowed back across the lake in comfortable laughter.

The afternoon sun hung low when they finally left the park and headed up Central Park West. Faith was giddy and exhausted.

"It must be over ninety." She mopped her brow with the back of her hand. Faith was seldom troubled by the heat, but now even the pink cotton crocheted top she'd chosen because it looked so crisp and cool felt hot as a blanket.

"The weather report I heard said it was going up to ninety-eight," Nick informed her. "We're in for quite a heat wave."

"Thank God for air conditioning." Faith watched Becky skip gracefully ahead of them, leading the ever-enthusiastic Figaro. "Where does she get her energy?"

"Kids are immune to heat, cold, rain and other discomforts. You'll find out." Nick's arm came casually around Faith's shoulders.

Remarkable how natural it felt, Faith thought. As if they'd always been friends, not adversaries.

"That's a very pensive smile," he commented.

"If you must know, I was thinking how easy you are to talk to."

"Tool of the trade," Nick said lightly, but the reference to his job made Faith tense. She was part of his work, just a story. She'd almost forgotten that.

She came out of her dream world abruptly and looked around her.

"Oh!" She had passed her block and walked up into the Seventies; now they had halted in front of an impressive marble-fronted building. Nick reached into his pocket for his keys.

Faith laughed nervously. "My goodness, I've come out of my way. I'll just take Figaro and go back. . . ."

"Oh, can't he stay? For a minute?" Becky pleaded, just as Nick said, "At least come in for a drink."

Faith looked at the two earnest faces and sighed.

"I want to take Figaro to meet Anne Marie," Becky said. "Is that okay?"

Faith remembered that Becky was new in the neighborhood, and a sheepdog was a good way to make friends. She nodded.

Nick smiled gratefully and led Faith inside, past a deferential doorman, across a marble lobby. Although she tried to look noncommittal, Faith was impressed. Her family's brownstone, bought with Cecily's money at a time when real estate was far cheaper, was now quite a valuable property, but Nick's co-op was luxurious. His duplex apartment occupied the two top floors of the building, and was furnished in simple but exquisite style.

Faith walked into the square, bay-windowed living room and gasped with pleasure.

"It's beautiful!" she said, and although Nick only said, "Make yourself comfortable," she could tell that he was pleased.

Faith wandered admiringly from the Queen Anne cherry tables to the tapestry wing chairs to the jade-green velvet Chesterfield sofa. Every detail was perfect. The carpet was a stunning Persian in green and red. Dominating the room was a large canvas which hung over the sofa. The swirls of greenish-blue and splashes of pink proclaimed it a late Monet—and original.

Faith stood transfixed before the painting. Eventually she realized that Nick was standing behind her, holding two glasses. She knew that he, too, would never tire of looking at the delicate willows, the mysterious river.

"Monet painted that scene a dozen times," Nick said softly. "His fascination comes right off the canvas at you, doesn't it?"

"Remarkable. I'm speechless." Faith paused. "How on earth did you get this painting? A Monet is worth a fortune. . . ."

"It was a gift." Noticing Faith's raised eyebrows, Nick explained, "A reward, actually. I tracked down some Nazi war criminals here who had been in charge of one of the concentration camps and had them extradited to West Germany for trial. The gentleman who owned this painting happened to have been a survivor of that camp. He had no family left, so he willed the Monet to me. 'For seeing justice done,' he said. I was stunned."

"I should think so," Faith said reverently.

"It also gave me the collecting bug," Nick confessed. "I have a Picasso and a Matisse in the library, and I just picked up a small Degas for Becky's room. Would you like to see them?"

Faith followed him delightedly, enjoying Nick's pride in his home and appreciating its beauty and style. There were paintings all along the long hall which Nick called "the gallery," mostly landscapes by contemporary artists whose names were new to Faith. The library, with its walls of books and casement windows, its rolltop desk and leather recliner, was obviously Nick's office. There was a starkly modern white kitchen, which to Faith's practiced eye looked little-used; a smallish dining room with an elegant chandelier and a beautiful antique sideboard; an enclosed terrace which ran the full width of the building. The terrace sported some healthy plants, wicker furniture and a clutter of toys.

"The bedrooms are upstairs," Nick mentioned casually, but Faith demurred. She knew if she once entered Nick Justin's bedroom, its image would haunt her. Her dreams were restless enough as it was.

Faith went out onto the terrace and sat on the porch swing. Nick removed a large teddy bear from the seat and sat beside her.

"Your place is beautiful," she said, "and it's immaculate. How on earth do you keep up with the work?"

Nick laughed. "A housekeeper, my dear."

"Oh." Faith hadn't noticed anyone.

"Sarah's off on weekends."

"What about when you get out-of-town assignments? Does she stay and take care of Becky? I imagine that must happen a lot."

"Not as much as it used to," Nick replied. "I won't leave for more than two or three days at a time now, so I've stuck to stories pretty close to home. Makes for a change of pace."

Stories like the MWA dinner, Faith thought ruefully. A far cry from the pieces he'd done last year: refugee camps in Malaysia, gun-running in Angola, a dangerous sail up from Colombia to Miami tracking a boatload of cocaine. . . .

Nick put his arm around her shoulders and she jumped.

"Are you bored," she asked, trying to cover the uncomfortable pounding of her heart, "staying in your own backyard?"

"Sometimes. It's a tradeoff. I love having the time with Becky, but every now and then—" He shrugged. "We had a lead come in last week, for instance. A terrorist training camp in Bulgaria. God, I'd love to break that wide open. . . ."

"But you turned it down."

"Bad timing. When Becky's older, maybe I'll go on the road again. But now, she needs me around."

Faith, mesmerized by his eyes, forgot to censor her speech. "Why don't you just get married again?" she asked bluntly. "Then there'd always be someone to take care of Becky when those hot leads come in."

Nick laughed. For one terrible moment, Faith feared he thought she was making him an offer. She turned red.

"Oh, to be twenty again," he chided, "and life so uncomplicated." He ran a teasing finger around the underside of her chin. "I'm no matrimonial bargain, Fanny. Who wants a guy with a lousy temper and a worse track record, who's on the road half the year and has a six-year-old who needs full-time attention?"

"Poor Mr. Justin," Faith mocked. "Come off it. I've seen the way women flock around you."

"Oh, that," he said deprecatingly. "It's easy to find someone to sleep with. But for a commitment like marriage, especially when there are two high-powered careers to consider—"

He paused. "I like ambitious women. Hell-raisers. But the women I see have no time for kids, not right now, and they're pretty blunt about saying so. . . ."

Nick stopped and looked down at his hands, as if embarrassed at revealing so much about his private life.

"But surely, if they met Becky . . ." Faith hesitated. "I can't imagine a better walking advertisement for parenthood."

"No." His eyes were raw with the pain of an unhealed wound. "I forced a woman into motherhood once. Never again."

"Oh, Nick." Impulsively, Faith reached for his hand. "I'm so sorry."

"I never thought my marriage could turn out that way." His voice held all the passion and all the bitterness of the past ten years. "Cynthia and I loved each other so much once."

Faith said, "I know you did."

"We married right out of college. I guess that was a mistake, but who knew then? We were both going to set the world on fire." He grimaced. "Ironic, isn't it? If we'd both been a little less ambitious, maybe we'd still be together. Maybe she'd still be alive."

"Oh, Nick." Faith didn't know what to say.

"We were such kids." He shook his head. "We couldn't keep our hands off each other, and we had the same taste in books and music and art; we thought that meant we were compatible. Unfortunately, we were poles apart on some of the most important things. . . ."

"Like children?" Faith asked softly.

He nodded. "But the problems with Becky were only the last straw. The marriage had collapsed long before that—"

"When you got so successful and Cynthia didn't?" Faith asked, helping him along.

"Damn it, she was a success," Nick said with passion. "She just didn't believe it. Cynthia wanted the kind of celebrity I had, even though in her field it was almost impossible to attain."

He frowned. "I admit I didn't help the situation much. I was pretty hell-for-leather in those days. Cynthia was right that I didn't invest much time in our marriage. But all I wanted was for her to be a little happy for me, just a little bit—"

"But she was too jealous?"

"Yeah. Got so I couldn't do anything right, in her eyes. So I came home less and less." He drained his glass and set it down on a side table with an oddly final click. "She saw other men," he said, his face averted. "Quite a few."

"And what about you?" Faith asked before she could stop herself. "Did you see other women?"

"Not for a long time. I kept hoping. . . ." His voice disappeared and he began again. "I was the one with the romantic view of marriage," he said slowly as he stared southward at his dazzling view of midtown Manhattan without seeing it. "You know, one woman, forever and ever. . . . When I found out Cynthia was cheating—and I found out in the worst possible way—I took it rather badly."

He met Faith's questioning eyes and shrugged. "I started seeing someone just to get back at Cynthia," he admitted. "Pretty immature, huh? And of course it didn't work out."

"I'm sorry," Faith said, meaning that she was sorry for his pain; she wasn't sorry the affair hadn't succeeded. "And now?"

"Now?" He gave her the ghost of a smile. "Footloose and fancy-free, of course. The only woman in my life is four-foot-six and wears hair ribbons."

"Oh," Faith said, vaguely disappointed at his reply. She caught him studying her and grew nervous at the intent in his hazel eyes. "I'd better be going," she said nervously. "Do you think Becky will be long with Figaro?"

"Possibly days," Nick said blandly. "I should have

warned you, when she and Anne Marie get together it generally takes an act of Congress to separate them. I don't expect her back for hours."

"Hours?" Faith said weakly.

Nick glanced at his watch. "Probably by now Anne Marie's mom is settling them down to dinner. She's from the old school—convinced a poor helpless bachelor like me couldn't possibly feed Becky adequately, and she knows I'm left to my own devices on weekends."

He grinned shamelessly and Faith swallowed hard. "Hours, huh?" she repeated, and wondered what she had let herself in for. "You should have told me."

"I had an ulterior motive," Nick said, and put his arm around her.

"You did?" Faith saw the devilish glint in his eyes, a bit of green flashing in the hazel. Her heart began to slam painfully. Now that she had seen a side of Nick he rarely showed, the sexual tension between them was worse than ever.

How vulnerable she was! Faith felt invaded. Her awareness of Nick dominated her thoughts and flooded through her veins. And the more he shared with her, the more he touched her every waking thought until it seemed that she carried a part of Nick Justin with her wherever she went.

This frightened Faith, because her cool and logical mind could find no name for what was happening to her. She'd always prided herself on the way she'd organized her life, each neat compartment—the Foundation, friends, family, her writing—self-contained and perfectly managed, each given the proper amount of her time and energy. When Faith was at work, she thought about work. When she was with friends, she gave herself completely to them. Yet now, wherever she was, whatever she tried to do, there was always a pulse in her mind saying Nick, Nick, Nick. She'd lost track of the number of times lately when she'd found herself gazing off into the distance remembering the feeling of his hands on her body or the light in his eyes when he smiled. . . .

There she went again! Guiltily Faith pulled herself back into the present and found herself facing a rather amused man. "I'd love to know what you were thinking," he said lightly.

"I was wondering how I got myself into this," Faith blurted. "Marooned on a terrace with a super-sleuth."

"Marooned on a terrace with a man," he corrected. "That's far more dangerous."

The seductive purr in his voice sent a shiver through her. Nick inclined toward her—an inch or two—and Faith shrank, pulled her shoulders in protectively, felt her temperature begin to soar.

"I don't think you're so dangerous," she ventured bravely, but her wide, apprehensive eyes belied her. Nick smiled, picked up her clenched hands and caressed them gently until they were relaxed and open in his grasp.

"That's better," he said softly. Nick leaned over and kissed her, and against her better judgment Faith found herself kissing him back. I'm going to be seduced, she thought, and was amazed at how warm and mellow the idea made her.

"Fanny—"

Nick's face changed suddenly as he looked down at her left hand; he grew sharp and alert, almost a stranger. "Where's your ring?" he demanded.

Faith suddenly remembered how rude he could be. "None of your business," she returned, without even knowing what ring he meant.

"Don't tell me you finally got some sense in your head and called off your damn-fool engagement?"

Faith bristled with anger. She was not about to tell him that she had, indeed, broken the "damn-fool" engagement—she would not give him the satisfaction.

"That hardly deserves a reply," she said frostily.

Nick greeted her stiff, haughty response with a frustrated expletive. "I'll never understand how a sensitive, intelligent woman like you could be such an idiot when it comes to men!" he roared. "You and Harald Clinton—why, it's ridiculous!"

"Oh, is it really? By whose standards?"

"Any rational human being's," Nick retorted. "Oh, you two look as pretty as a perfume ad, but there's no real feeling there. I don't care if he's a terrific lover, you should know by now that he'll never make you happy—"

"How can you say that?" Faith demanded angrily. "You don't know—"

"I know you haven't even been able to tell him about your book." Nick looked disgusted. "Some honest relationship you've got."

"I did so tell him." Faith defended herself bravely but couldn't help remembering Harald's snide response to her disclosure.

"And?" Nick quickly saw the disappointment she struggled to hide. "What's the matter, wasn't *Blood Poisoning* good enough for him?"

How could Faith admit that Harald hadn't even believed she'd written the book? "He—um—wasn't exactly thrilled."

"Unsuitable behavior for the future Mrs. Congressman? And you actually want to marry this guy? Damn it, Fanny!" Nick said explosively. "Use your head! Clinton doesn't care about you—"

"Oh, really? Is that what your sources tell you?"

He hesitated just long enough so that Faith knew she had hit on the truth. "My God, I'm right!" she cried. "You've been investigating Harald!"

"I looked into a few things, that's all," Nick muttered. "I don't trust him. And neither should you."

"Is that so?" Faith was furious at his paternalistic attitude.

"Yes. And no matter how mad you are, you should listen. Before you find out the hard way."

"Find out what?" Faith asked, her curiosity stronger than her desire to snub him.

"He's got dirty money in his campaign. He's in the mob's pocket, Fanny. I can't prove it yet, but—you don't look surprised."

"I'm not," Faith said reluctantly. "I've worried about all the money. Harald seems to have so much to spend, and you know how rare that is in politics." She sighed. "Winning this race is so important to him, he'd do anything. I guess I hoped he was using family money—"

"It's family money, all right," Nick snorted. "Family like that you don't need."

"No." Faith looked at Nick's uneasy face and knew, sickeningly, that she had not heard the worst. "You're holding something back, aren't you? What?"

"Isn't that enough?" Nick asked, deliberately evasive. "You don't want Clinton, Fanny."

"You said," Faith said slowly, "that he didn't care about me. Those were your exact words. And you wouldn't say that, unless you knew something definite—"

She halted in midthought and let out a little cry. "Harald's having an affair, isn't he? Or two or three?"

She knew it was true before Nick spoke, knew it from the delicate way he avoided looking at her. She felt a flash of pain that surprised her.

"Don't marry him, Fanny." She was shocked at the violence in Nick's voice. "For God's sake, don't marry that—" He stopped, as if at last recalling that Faith presumably loved the man. "Sleep with him if you want to, but—"

"I don't want to." Faith blurted the words without thinking of the consequences. "I haven't wanted to since—"

She heard herself then and stopped in horror.

"Since when?" Nick prompted, his voice electric. Faith stared at the floor with her face in flames.

"You know perfectly well when," she muttered.

Nick sat down beside her, took her in his arms. Her bones melted as he turned her face up to his. "Tell me."

Faith knew she would never forget the look on Nick's face: overpowering, intense yearning; an eagerness that he was trying hard to suppress; a hint of shyness that melted her heart in the most devastating fashion, simply because any sign of vulnerability in him was so unexpected.

"Tell me when," he begged, as he took her face between his hands, and Faith was helpless to conceal her thoughts.

"Since the night I met you," she confessed in a whisper. "Since you kissed me—"

The memories flooded back then, as Nick's knowing hands found the sensitive flesh at the back of her neck, his touch feathering up into her hair as he brought her mouth to his. Memories of a cab halted under a lamp-post, and a kiss that had shocked them both with its passion. . . .

Funny, Faith thought, that she could still feel that shock every time Nick touched her. She should be used to him by now, but the pleasure of his lips hard against hers, his tongue plunging deep inside her mouth, was as wild and fresh as it had been that night.

But she had changed. Now, instead of trying to suppress her feelings, Faith let them have free rein. She let her hands play up the back of Nick's shirt and bury themselves in the sensuous fullness of his chestnut hair. Faith savored the contrasts there, under her fingers: the silk of his hair, the sandpaper texture of his strong jaw, the surprising softness in the triangular hollow at the base of his throat. . . . She followed her instincts and kissed him there, and heard Nick's low sound of pleasure, felt his suddenly exhaled breath rippling her hair.

"Witch," he whispered as his lips traveled down her hairline. "Don't you know how much I want you?"

He kissed her with a complete passion that devastated her senses. Faith curled against Nick happily and let him touch her at will. His hands, driven by instinct as old as time, quickly found their way under her sweater and up to the round fullness of her breasts. She gasped.

"There's something different about you today," he murmured between kisses, as he fingered the lace edge of Faith's bra in a tempting, almost-but-not-quite caress that nearly drove her insane. "You seem so—"

He paused to nibble on her earlobe. "Free," he finished.

I am free, Faith thought, free of Harald. While she had been engaged, Faith had always felt a duty to fight her desire for Nick. She would never have dared, for instance, to take Nick's hand and press it tightly to her swelling breast, as she did now without even thinking about it.

"Well, Fanny?" Nick demanded hoarsely. "Are you free?"

"Yes," she breathed, as she pulled his body even closer to hers. "I—"

"Thank God."

"Oh, Nick—" Her words were lost in the onslaught of his mouth. "No—I—"

She gave up the effort to talk and clung to Nick dizzily while his tongue flicked deeper and deeper into the sweetness of her mouth. He pulled her down beneath him and let her feel the hard outline of his body beneath his jeans, the force of his desire for her.

"Let me make love to you, Fanny," he whispered, and she felt a quiver run down into her pelvis. "I want you so—"

"You do?" she asked innocently, wide-eyed, and he answered her with a fierce, passionate caress that ran the full length of her body and extinguished any doubt in her mind.

"God, don't you know that I've wanted you ever since I first saw you?"

"Oh," she murmured, her mind paralyzed.

"Is that all you can say?" Nick asked softly.

"Well, I-I . . ." She hung back, unable to speak the words that would give herself to him.

"Are you afraid?" he asked suddenly, and his voice was unbelievably gentle. Faith nodded, ashamed of her childish behavior. "Why?" he asked, troubled, as he cradled her close against him. "You must know that I would never hurt you."

Now, she found that easy to believe, and told him so.

"Then why? It's hard to believe you don't want me when you hold me and kiss me like that—"

"Don't want you?" Faith's voice was low and unintentionally sultry. "If I wanted you any more I'd probably die from it." She looked up at him from under her lashes, her blue eyes huge in her heart-shaped face. "But I've never felt like this before, and it scares me. Can't you see that?" she whispered. "Don't you have any heart at all?"

"Feel this," he said as he took her hand and placed it under his shirt, against his chest. Faith felt the heavy thud of his heart beneath her fingers. Her own heart began to race in answer. She looked up at him and the air between them crackled with anticipation.

"Oh, Nick," Faith moaned, and she felt any sensible thought she'd ever had slipping away from her. There was only feeling, feeling too strong to be mastered.

The words came out without her willing them. "Kiss me."

He did—a wild, devouring kiss that destroyed whatever was left of Faith's conscious mind. His hands moved passionately over the contours of breast and hip and thigh until neither of them could bear to be separated by even so flimsy a barrier as her light sweater.

Nick rose impatiently, and swung Faith up into his arms.

"I'm taking you to bed," he said, and carried a startled Faith up the steps to his bedroom.

8

She should have said no, then, she wasn't ready for this. But somehow, as they stood together in the fading sunlight of Nick's bedroom and he sensuously slipped first her sweater and then her jeans from her trembling body, Faith couldn't manage to say a word.

Nick pulled back the comforter and laid her gently in the center of his huge bed. As he stared down at her, the yearning on his face nearly broke her heart. No man had ever looked at Faith with such passionate tenderness. Seeing it, she could deny him nothing.

Nick lay down beside her and touched her hair, softly, as if she were fragile and might break. Faith closed her eyes and waited. Then she realized that Nick was unfastening her hair, pulling the pins out and releasing her long locks one by one. His fingers followed each strand down as it fell across her breasts and shoulders and back, turning each simple movement into a provocative caress.

"You have beautiful hair, Fanny," he whispered. "Like a sun that never sets." He reached beneath the golden curtain to cup her breast, now hidden from him by only a wisp of lace. Impatiently Nick unhooked the clasp of her bra and released her breasts into his hands. Faith gasped as his fingers found her taut nipples and flicked them back and forth. Her flesh swelled and surged against him.

"Nick, no—"

"Yes." He held her gaze as his hand slid possessively lower, searching out the hollow of her hip, the rounded curve of her outer thigh. He explored her calf, her ankle, even pressed a kiss into the arch of her foot until Faith felt that no particle of her was secret from him.

She understood then. He meant to have all of her, every inch.

Faith trembled as his hands worked their way back up her body, discovering the sensitive hollow at the back of her knees, lingering over the still more dangerous flesh of her inner thighs. His maddening fingers moved even higher, and pulled down the silk of her bikini underpants. Faith brushed his hand away.

"Nick, no, please—I can't—"

As he kissed her protests into silence, his hand returned again and again, until Faith had no will left to stop him. And once he reached her moist interior she couldn't have borne it if he had stopped. Faith felt her resistance breaking down, snapping like so many overstressed strings. She could hide nothing from him, not even the embarrassed little whimpers of pleasure that betrayed how completely she had succumbed to his touch.

"You blush all over your body."

Even with her eyes closed, Faith knew Nick was smiling. Blindly she reached for his head and cradled it in the valley between her breasts while she struggled to regain control of her breathing. But he would not stay still; he moved against her, tormenting her, his mouth tantalizing the peaks of her breasts until she cried out his name. And another word. "Please—"

Nick rolled over on his side and looked down at her, his eyes shimmering green in the fading light. "I knew you would look like that," he whispered hoarsely. "Sensuous and wild."

Sensuous? she thought. Wild? *Her?* And then she saw his face, and she had to believe him.

He's going to make love to me, Faith told herself, dazed with disbelief. She watched Nick's fingers shake as he stripped off his clothing, heard his moan as he lay down beside her and their flesh touched, length to length, for the first time.

"God, you feel so good—"

Had she said that? Or had he? No matter, they reached for each other in the same instant and kissed with a hunger that fused them into one being, as if they were sculpture cut from a single block of marble.

"Oh, God." Nick sounded as if he were strangling. "Fanny, you are so beautiful. . . ."

"So are you," she whispered. She touched the rippling muscles of Nick's back as he lifted himself to position his body over hers. For a moment Nick looked at her, and Faith knew she would always remember the sight of him, poised above her, the sunset light turning his body to fire.

"I want you." Nick's rough, hot, out-of-control voice thrilled her body and soul. "Now—"

"Then take me," she whispered. But he didn't, not until she was dizzy with need and nearly insensible with desire. When he entered her Faith felt as if she were melting, splitting in two, yet she arched against him, willing him even deeper inside her, carried away by her own pleasure. And then she found out the pleasure was only beginning.

Faith's cascading emotions stunned her, as did the

sudden, utter waywardness of her body. She couldn't stop her legs from sliding up Nick's thighs and locking around his hips, or stop herself from moving maddeningly, rhythmically, as if her body had a will of its own. She couldn't stop moaning, wild little animal cries that inflamed Nick to even greater passion than she had guessed possible. By the end she was merely a shuddering mass of sensation, a vessel of liquid fire. She felt the climax build inside her and tried but failed to choke back the sound rising in her throat. Helpless, Faith turned her head and her cry was muffled in the pillow.

Overwhelmed, Faith pressed her face into the sheets for a long while afterward, in no state to notice that Nick was as shattered as she. But moments later, he still drew great shuddering breaths as he nestled beside her and clasped her fiercely against him. He muttered an undecipherable word that might have been "Mine . . ."

Faith didn't hear. She was too shocked by the words that had sprung to her own lips, words that only her utter breathlessness had prevented Nick from hearing.

She had whispered, "I love you. . . ."

Could that be true?

Faith feared it was—that now, with all her defenses down, she had finally seen into her own heart. She loved Nick Justin, had probably loved him since she first saw him. And now he certainly must know.

Faith had never felt so in danger, so at risk. She burrowed her head into his chest and wished that time would stop. Nick held her quietly and stroked her hair and waited for the tension to pass out of her body.

"Fanny," he whispered into her hair. "Tell me how you feel."

"I feel wonderful," she said, in so forlorn a voice that he laughed.

"We're wonderful together," he replied easily. "Don't you think?"

"I can't think. I'm too scared."

"Scared? Why?" His voice sharpened with guilt. "Did I hurt you? I know I got rather . . . intense—"

"No, you didn't hurt me, silly." Faith spoke quickly when she saw the concern on his face. "It's just . . ." She wished she hadn't looked at him, hadn't seen the passion in his now-greenish hazel eyes, or the contented complacency with which he handled her body. As if she belonged to him now more than she belonged to herself.

"Just what?" He paused, and Faith found herself wishing fervently that Nick would say something. Not "I love you." She couldn't hope for that, but something to take their lovemaking out of the realm of the purely casual encounter.

But those words didn't come, and Faith wasn't bold enough to be the first to speak. "Nothing," she murmured.

Nick seemed about to press the issue, but his respect for Faith's private emotions restrained him. Instead he stroked every part of her body and whispered soft words that were somehow both sexy and comforting.

Only later did Faith realize that she had somehow drifted off to sleep in his arms. She woke, drowsy and contented, with one hand on Nick's shoulder and the other curled in astounding intimacy around his thigh.

Startled, Faith tried to sneak her hand away. Nick chuckled and Faith's hand was firmly returned to an even more intimate location.

At her shocked gasp Nick laughed easily, and Faith found herself laughing too. Nick pulled her on top of him, and her hair swung down into his face. "Feeling better now?"

"I feel divine," Faith gasped as his mouth found her breast. "I—oh . . ."

"And how is that?"

"That's marvelous, and you know it." Faith stared at

him with a spark of her old defiance, but the warmth in his eyes took her breath away. She touched her fingers lightly to the crinkling lines of pleasure around Nick's eyes and mouth, and felt a surge of love for him so strong she couldn't breathe.

"And to think," she murmured, "how terrified I once was of the great Nick Justin."

"Why?" He nibbled casually on her neck.

"Because of your story, silly." Faith snuggled down next to him and snaked her fingers lovingly up the hair on his chest.

"The MWA story?" There was a sharper note in his voice but Faith was in no condition to hear it.

"What else?" She sighed and kissed his collarbone, ran her fingers possessively along the strongly defined muscles of his chest. "When I think how close you came to ruining my life! If you would have run that story—"

His body stiffened under her touch. "What are you saying? That now I won't?"

Faith heard it then—a note of iron, cold and hard, in the voice that had been so caressing. But she ignored its warning, because she'd heard something that, momentarily, frightened her even more.

Not a statement: "Now I won't," but a question. As if the *Newsview* story were still hanging over her head, as if he were still threatening to expose her.

"Of course you won't run the story," she said, her voice quick and crisp to cover her fear that, indeed, he might. "How could you—now?"

"What do you mean, 'now'?"

Faith heard the effort it took him to keep his voice level. "Now that we're"—she struggled over the word—"lovers."

"My God," Nick said in a chilling voice. He pulled away from her as if she were diseased. "So that's what's been going on here. A little bribe."

She saw the shuttered look come over his face, closing her out, and words rushed out of her in panic. "Nick, you couldn't run that story now! Not knowing all about me, what it would do to me! Not after—you couldn't be that cruel!"

"You're a fine one to talk about being cruel, lady," he rasped, and vaulted out of the bed. "Damn you."

Nick pulled on his jeans so violently that Faith flinched. "I should have known," he muttered. "I should have known."

"Known what?" she cried in distress.

"About you." Nick's contempt stung like a whip. He looked at her, and Faith, suddenly afraid of what she read in his face, clutched the comforter up around her breasts. "Hell, I did know, but you were so damn beautiful I didn't want to believe it."

His fist pounded the windowsill with such force the panes rattled. "I'm only human. And I wanted you. God help me—"

"I don't understand—" she began timidly, and he cut her off with a curse.

"At least spare me this innocent act, Fanny. Or haven't you had enough? Do you want to see just how much you can make me bleed?"

Faith knew, then, that things had gone beyond reclaiming and she scrambled out of the bed and reached for her clothes.

"I'm sorry," she muttered, not actually sure what she apologized for. She pulled on her wispy lace underwear with fingers that trembled. "I never meant to hurt you."

He strode to her and seized her shoulders. "Oh, no, you never meant to hurt me. Well, that's what happens when you use people, Fanny. They get hurt."

"Use . . . you?" Faith echoed in utter bewilderment.

"Oh, don't look so innocent. Remember that you're sitting on my bed—and the whole time you were in it all you cared about was keeping that damn story off the air!"

Faith saw then, and her heart sank. "No!"

"That's all you've ever cared about, where I'm concerned." He threw her jeans at her and she tugged them on, feeling that she couldn't get dressed fast enough. "You tried to run away from me and when that didn't work, you told me your whole sad story and tried to work on my sympathy to get what you wanted."

Faith bent down to pick up her sweater. His relentless voice followed her. "And then you befriended my daughter, so I'd feel too indebted to you to cause you any trouble. And when all else failed, you decided to go to bed with me—"

"That's not true!" Faith cried.

"Oh, really?" Nick stood, feet planted, arms akimbo, unmistakably challenging her. His naked torso shone with sweat and his jeans clung to his slim hips. Faith felt a surge of desire for him so strong it rocked her back and forth. Shocking, that even now, when he hated her, while he was willfully misunderstanding her and devaluing her soul, she could fantasize about Nick picking her up and throwing her across his bed.

"It's one of the more enjoyable bribes I've received in my time," Nick continued witheringly. "But the story airs just the same."

"Fine, damn you," Faith shouted, as furious with her own thoughts as she was with Nick. "If you're such a fool you think that's all I care about—"

"You made it pretty obvious, lady. You made one mistake, though. You shouldn't have mentioned the story so soon. I was so dazzled by your performance I might not have seen through you for weeks."

He stalked out of the room and Faith chased down the steps after him, calling out words she'd never said aloud in her life before. She glared at him in fury. "You've made up your mind that all women are scheming and not to be trusted, so you put the worst possible interpretation on everything I say and do. By God, I could sprout wings and a halo and you still wouldn't believe me. Well, to hell with it, Mr. Justin. I'm through trying to justify myself to you. You can do your story and be damned." And Faith marched out of the apartment.

"And then he said I was trying to seduce him so that he wouldn't televise the story." Faith pulled a casserole out of the oven and set the steaming dish gingerly on the table. "Me seduce him! Can you believe that?"

"Stranger things have happened," Bonnie replied calmly with a twinkle in her eye. "I say bravo."

"You have no pity at all, do you?" Faith sighed.

"I think Nick Justin's the best thing that ever happened to you."

"Past tense," Faith corrected. "I've been trying to tell you, he hates the sight of me."

"You exaggerate, surely."

"You didn't see his face. He could have killed me."

"But that's good, Faith. It means you matter to him, don't you see?" Bonnie waved her spoon in emphasis. "It's indifference that's the kiss of death."

"But I've botched the whole thing! He was just beginning to trust me—and my Lord, Bonnie, he's such a wonderful lover—and now I've ruined it all, just because I mentioned his damn story!"

Faith realized she was slipping into incoherence, and bitterly stabbed a fork into her casserole. "I wonder why he's so determined to believe I can't be trusted. There's a Spanish proverb that says, 'The wedge that hurts most is the one from the same tree.'"

"You mean, Nick is extra-suspicious that you're putting on an act for him, because all the while he's putting on an act for *you?*"

"Makes sense, doesn't it?" Faith asked. "He's hyper-sensitive about my motives, because all the while he's making love to me, all he wants is grist for his story."

"I don't believe that," Bonnie argued. "Sounds like a lot of work to go to for just a story."

"You're so romantic," Faith said. "Can you really see us together? The champion cynic and the last Victorian in New York?"

"Opposites attract," Bonnie said peaceably. "The man's obviously in love with you."

Faith greeted this optimistic statement with an uncharitable one-word reply.

"You can't tell me he treats all his subjects this way," Bonnie said.

"He'd be drummed off the air if he did."

"Well, then, his interest must be personal."

"Sheer lust," Faith said. "If anything."

"Faith, wake up. The man cares about you. He cares a lot."

"He has a hell of a way of showing it," Faith grumbled. "And I bet it's the same old story. I'm Harrison Daniels' daughter. It's Daddy he's fascinated with, not me."

"Bull," Bonnie said succinctly. "That first night, at the banquet, when he chased you all over town—he had no idea you were Harrison Daniels' daughter. He fell for Fanny Duvall."

"Bonnie, that's even worse! Don't you see? He wants a woman who doesn't exist!"

"Doesn't she?" Bonnie asked.

Faith groaned. They finished the meal in silence.

"Isn't it about time we fed Figaro?" Bonnie asked after they finished the dishes. "Where is the great beast?"

"Oh, my Lord," Faith breathed. "I left him."

"Left him? Where?"

Faith turned to her roommate with anguished eyes. "In the dragon's den."

"With Justin?"

"With Becky, actually." And Faith explained how she'd been parted from her dog.

"Well, you have to go back and get him," Bonnie said sensibly.

"Oh, no. I couldn't. How can I?"

Bonnie smiled at Faith's woebegone face. "Cheer up. Maybe Nick will bring Figaro back for you."

"If he does, I'm not home. Tell him I committed myself to Bellevue."

"You should see him, Faith." But at the look on Faith's face, Bonnie relented. "All right, but what if he doesn't believe me? He's got a suspicious nature, remember?"

Faith groaned again.

Not fifteen minutes later came an imperious ring at the downstairs intercom, accompanied by a familiar bark. Faith fled to her bedroom and shut the door. Sounds came faintly through the wood: happy barking, Bonnie's throaty alto, Nick's baritone grating in reply. Faith sighed. The edge of his afternoon's anger lingered in his voice.

The barking increased in volume, then gave way to a snuffle and a whine. Faith heard Figaro scratch against her door. She gave up, opened the door, and gathered the shaggy bulk into her arms.

"Thank you for returning Figaro," Faith told Nick in a stiff and formal voice. She couldn't bear to look into his eyes.

"Not at all. Becky enjoyed him immensely." Nick was doing his best to sound as if they were strangers.

"Good." As the silence lengthened, Faith wondered why Nick did not leave. They stood and stared at each other, like fighters in the ring waiting for the starting bell. Bonnie took one look at them and vanished quietly into the kitchen.

Faith broke first. "Is there something you wanted to say to me?"

"Many things, Miss Daniels, but I'll let most of them pass." His voice rasped across Faith's nerves like nails on a blackboard.

"Good. I've more important things to do than be lectured by a frustrated sadist."

"I've come to inform you I'll be interviewing your friends and coworkers this week to get material for my profile. I thought you might like to let them know."

"You wouldn't!" Faith cried, and thought, He's only doing this to punish me.

"Try me," Nick said roughly. "I'll ask them about *Blood Poisoning,* of course, so you might want to break the news about your book. Of course, if you don't tell them, that's fine—I'll be glad to. Might make for better television that way."

"You're a skunk," Faith said.

"Oh, come on, you can do better than that. Try."

"I'm too much of a lady."

"When did that transformation take place?" Nick demanded.

"Oh!" Faith seethed with fury. "You are the lowest, most contemptible . . ." Her words trailed off as he slouched against the arm of her sofa. Nick still wore the shirt and jeans he'd worn in the afternoon, and the sight of his body, in those clothes, made her throb with desire.

"I would have thought the great Nick Justin was above taking revenge," she finished.

"Revenge?" He gave a hollow laugh. "This comes under the heading of social work."

"Oh, I see. You'll ruin my life out of the goodness of your heart."

"You don't need me to ruin your life, lady," Nick snapped back. "You've done a great job all by yourself. And when you finally do something halfway worthwhile, you don't have the guts to follow through—"

"Since when," Faith demanded, "is sharing your bed

one of the highest and best goals of womanhood? You flatter yourself."

"I was referring," Nick said coldly, "to your book."

"Oh." Color flooded Faith's cheeks.

"Do you know what your problem is? You're suffering from a prolonged adolescence. Fanny, you're not a baby anymore. You don't need to be protected from life. If you want to write, write. If you want to work at the Foundation, then do it. But stop all these charades and take responsibility for your actions. For God's sake, grow up!"

Nick left before Faith could frame a suitable reply.

Even the next morning, as Faith sat on her familiar bench in the gazebo, Nick's words echoed through her mind. Faith gazed out over the calm waters, her mind conjuring an image of herself in a rowboat. She wore a rather Edwardian white dress and picture hat; across from her sat Nick Justin, his powerful arms sweeping the oars through the water.

Faith shook off the image. Her life had been so much easier when she saw Nick as a magnetic, dangerous adversary, a Mephistopheles determined to lead her to perdition. But since Saturday, even before they'd made love, Faith had been forced to see him differently. As a man. Complex, formidable, moody, yes, but forthright, loyal, kind, honest. A man capable of deep love—one had only to watch him with Becky to see that—and surprising tenderness.

And something more. A man who needed a woman in his life. Faith remembered the beautiful apartment as full of uninhabited space, hungering for a woman's presence. She was haunted by memories of their lovemaking, memories of the picnic on the riverbank. Here, she suddenly knew, was a man who had never been loved as he deserved, a man who needed, would thrive on, that love.

But not with her. Never with her, now.

Faith tossed her notebook into her shoulder bag and summoned Figaro to her side impatiently. The day was already insufferably hot. Faith sighed. The weather forecasters' dire predictions of more than one-hundred-degree temperatures seemed destined to come true.

Seeking a breeze, Faith walked down the bank to a spot where a willow dipped its long graceful stalks into the water. The wafting of the branches stirred the stifling air. Faith sank down to the bank, her arm around Figaro's neck.

"Do you know what your problem is? You're suffering from a prolonged adolescence."

Nick's words drummed again and again in her ears.

Faith pried loose a pebble from the ground and flung the stone out into the pond. Nick was right about her. She still craved approval from Prue more than anything in the world, had been willing to sacrifice her independence, her own identity, to win her aunt's love. She'd gone to work at the Foundation simply to please Prue, and accepted Harald's proposal because Prue approved the match.

Another pebble followed the first. Prolonged adolescence indeed. Faith looked at her life with her new, adult's eyes and was appalled at her choices. She didn't like working at the Foundation, had never liked it.

And Harald! When she contrasted him with Nick's intelligence and vitality she could scarcely label them both the same species!

Faith had a sudden tormenting vision of herself in Nick's arms, naked, making love.

"I do love him," she whispered into Figaro's thick fur. "I do. And now I've ruined it all."

There was no doubt about that. Having lost Nick's good opinion for the second time, what chance was there that he would ever trust her again?

9

Faith didn't know when she had made up her mind to try to see Nick again. The idea just emerged, rock-hard and certain in her consciousness, until it was impossible for her to think of anything else.

She had a dozen different justifications—Nick had her Edgar award, which she could use as proof of her authorship when she told Prue why she was leaving the Foundation; she could tell Nick she was going public about her book and didn't care any longer if he ran his damn story—but in her heart Faith knew only one reason mattered. She wanted to see the man she loved, to hear his voice even if he taunted her, to tell him she was leaving the Foundation and watch his quick, approving smile.

For a moment Faith wondered if she had merely substituted one master for another. Her desire for Nick's acceptance—wasn't that just as bad as slaving to win Prue's approval all these years?

But no. Faith saw that Nick's attitude toward her was different from Prue or Harald's. Nick had no image she must conform to; he only pressed her to follow her heart. In her twenty-three years, no one but Nick and Bonnie had ever urged Faith to be herself, and she could not now bear to part with either of them. She would fight to regain Nick's regard.

Perhaps they could be friends.

Where would Nick be now? Faith wondered. Home with Becky? Out of town? On a date? Working? Faith took a guess, dug out the crumpled business card he had given her, and dialed his private office number.

The line was busy. Even at seven-thirty on a torrid Sunday night in June, Nick Justin was working.

"That settles it," Faith told Bonnie, with more assurance than she actually felt. "I'm going to his office."

"This late?" Bonnie asked. "Why not wait a bit and try to catch him at his place? It's more—private."

"No, I'd rather do this in a business setting," Faith said stubbornly. "Keep the discussion on a civil plane."

"Whatever you say," Bonnie replied. "But you look more like you're ready to go dancing with Fred Astaire than talk business."

Faith adjusted the delicate halter top of her full-skirted white dress. "Nonsense," she said, as she clipped on a necklace of coral and tiny freshwater pearls. "I'm only wearing this because it's the coolest thing I own. In case you haven't noticed, it's one hundred and two degrees out there—"

"Let's hope it doesn't get hotter," Bonnie returned.

Faith made a face at her, picked up her purse, and ran downstairs to hail a cab.

Twenty minutes later Faith was in an elevator at network headquarters, rocketing up to Nick's office on the thirty-ninth floor, having breezed by the security officer with a quick nod. Rapid defiance of gravity was not the only force making her stomach turn over and over. Faith rehearsed, again, what she would say.

Nick had her Edgar award; she needed it back. Why? And then Faith would give him an airy smile, as if it were nothing, and announce that she was going public about her book, and wanted the Edgar to back up her claim to be Fanny Duvall.

Perfectly plausible. Unimpeachable.

Still, Faith shook as she got off the elevator. The receptionist's desk on thirty-nine was empty, the corridors silent and dim.

Funny, Faith had expected the news department of a major television network to be bustling with people. Then she realized this was an executive floor, all posh private offices. The news department proper, with its ever-ringing telephones and its hive of scurrying reporters, was two floors below her. The thirty-ninth floor—as she passed closed door after closed door—was deserted.

Faith's confidence evaporated. To approach Nick Justin in a cluttered, hyperactive newsroom, surrounded by his colleagues, was one thing; it was quite another to tackle him alone.

She rapped hesitantly at his door.

"Come in."

Faith winced at the grating voice, but obeyed instructions.

"What the hell do you want?" The dark head looked up from a video display terminal. The tone was not friendly.

Faith gulped. "I've come to claim my property."

"What, did you leave your bra under my bed?"

She reddened. Nick was going to be difficult. Her sweet fantasies of reconciliation punctured and faded away.

"No. You have my Edgar. I want it back."

He sat back in his swivel chair and crossed his arms. She had surprised him. "Really? Why, may I ask?"

Her carefully prepared explanation withered on her tongue. "It's mine," she said with childish stubbornness. "I want to have it."

He lifted an eyebrow. "What sort of terms are you offering?"

"You—!" Faith stammered in fury. "You have no right to keep my property! And how dare you suggest that I would—"

A booming laugh silenced her, and Faith realized that he was teasing her. "You're a rat, Nick Justin," she muttered.

"First a skunk, now a rat; you're running down the whole animal kingdom," he said easily. "Have a seat, Fanny, and tell me what's going on. I take it you are Fanny tonight?"

She sat on his sofa without replying.

Nick leaned forward. "You've decided to go public about *Blood Poisoning,* haven't you?"

"Yes," she admitted.

"Why?" His voice was casual. Faith did not notice the heightened intensity in the hazel eyes.

"You know perfectly well why. I'm being railroaded into it."

"Aha. My fault again."

Faith shrugged. "No, it's not your fault," she said, ever fair. "It had to come. Your story just rushed things a bit." Faith swallowed, her eyes glued to the scarlet carpet. "But I'd like to have the Edgar with me when I tell my aunt. Just as moral support."

Nick rose. "If it's proof you're after, why don't you show her this?" He led Faith down the hall and into a small screening room. She stood, confused, as he puttered among the video cassettes and placed one in a projector and turned the monitor on.

"Here. Proof incontrovertible that you are Fanny Duvall." He clicked off the lights and the video ran in silence.

The Plaza. Awards night. Faith grinned as she saw Nick, all sharp angles and starched white shirt. Then various luminaries in the crowd, on the dais. Herself and Ken Powell, at a private table, laughing. Ken was holding her hand. Faith frowned. She had not realized how intimate their relationship looked. She shot a glance over at Nick, but his face was shuttered, unreadable in the flickering light.

Then Faith was on the dais, accepting her award. She had forgotten the sweetness of this moment in the crashing aftermath of that night; now it was as if Nick had given her victory back to her to cherish, whole and unblemished.

She watched the slim figure in the ice-blue dress and a tide of emotion engulfed her. Her hunger for acceptance jumped off the screen. How vulnerable she looked. How young.

The video cut to a reaction shot of Nick: his face was open, his eyes naked with compassion. Faith had seldom seen such raw emotion in his previous stories, except when he'd cradled a child dying of hunger in east Africa. No wonder his cameraman had lingered, fascinated, on his face.

If only I had worn my glasses that night, Faith thought ruefully. I would have seen that look, and known him for a friend, not an enemy.

But there was no way to stop the rush of events. The video ran on. Nick accosted Faith, microphone in hand, and the succeeding interview brought Faith nothing but pain. She had been brittle, terrified, hostile; now she saw that Nick's rough questions, his relentless harassment, had sprung from a defense mechanism. Nick had been touched by her, perhaps attracted, so he would be extra-tough in his interrogation lest his partiality show.

Fool, fool, fool, Faith screamed to herself. If you had only known.

The video flickered to an end and died. They sat in silence, lost in private thoughts, while Nick rewound the cassette. With a tact she hadn't suspected he possessed, Nick left her alone to compose herself while he put the cassette away. When he'd finished, Faith rose and mutely followed him back to his office.

Nick's patience lasted only that long. He snapped on the lamp beside the sofa. "What's wrong, Fanny?" he demanded. "You look like you've been through hell."

Watching that film had been a bit like walking through hell: seeing her mistakes mount up, one by one, mistakes that would cost her the only man she'd ever loved.

"It's that damn story," Faith said, and watched his face grow tense. "Now, don't jump on me," she added warningly, "I'm not disputing your right to air it. I just—it makes me sad."

"Why?" Nick sat on the arm of the sofa, his arm braced against the wall mere inches from Faith's head. The nearness of his body sent a wave of sensual awareness through her; her heart fluttered.

"Because it reminds me of all the mistakes I made with you," she confessed. "Makes me see what a coward I've been all my life. And I'm so ashamed of myself—"

He cut across her words impatiently. "There's no need—"

"Yes, there is," she continued stubbornly. "I've behaved like a baby. But," she added, "there's one thing I'm not guilty of."

"And what's that?"

"Making love to you so that you'd kill the story." Even in the dim light of the single lamp Faith could see a flush spread over Nick's cheekbones. "You've been right about the rest of my failings, but not that. Never that. I could never give myself to a man for any reason except . . ."

Her voice faltered over the words "loving him," and Faith censored herself just in time. "Wanting him," she substituted shyly, and blushed.

Nick interrupted her. "But yesterday, you said—"

"I know what I said—that you wouldn't do the story—but that was just wishful thinking on my part. I certainly wasn't trying to pressure you to drop the story." Faith sighed. "I would never interfere in your work. I thought you knew that. I guess I just hoped that you'd care enough for me. . . ."

"I do care." His voice was so quiet Faith had to watch his lips move to be certain he had spoken. "But killing the story—letting you hide under a bushel for a few more years—that wouldn't be doing you any favors, Fanny." He clenched his fingers and forcibly relaxed them. "I know you think I've been persecuting you, but that wasn't my intention. I just wanted you to—"

"Grow up," Faith finished. "So you've said. And I hated you for it."

"I know." A fleeting smile crossed Nick's face and vanished. "And now?"

"Now?" Faith lost her courage when he sat next to her, much too close. "I-I don't know."

His arm came around her shoulders. "Haven't you forgiven me, Fanny?" His mouth came down on hers.

The kiss was gentle, playful, affectionate. Clearly Nick was affirming friendship, not intending to arouse her, but Faith stirred against him anyway, her hands slipping up to lose themselves in his soft hair. When he let her go her eyes glistened.

Nick's hand cupped her jaw, his fingers against the pulse in her throat.

Something happened to the light. Nick hadn't bothered to turn on the fluorescent ceiling fixtures; only the table lamp by the sofa was lit. Now, beneath its white shade, the bulb turned red, bright red. Faith gasped and pointed.

"What's wrong with the light?" As Nick turned, the bulb slowly glowed white again.

"Power drain. And no wonder. Every air conditioner in New York must be on."

Faith shivered. "It's spooky. I thought the bulb was going to blow out."

"Let's save it the trouble." Nick reached over and clicked off the light. Faith's heart jumped. They sat in the glow of the single, floor-to-ceiling window that was the south wall of Nick's office, bathed in moonlight and the scattered lights of skyscrapers. The far-off windowpanes shone like a thousand yellow stars. There was no sound but the hum of the air conditioner and the hammering of Faith's heart. She waited for Nick to kiss her again. Surely that's what he intended—

"Fanny?" His fingers stroked up and down her bare shoulders, setting off explosions along her nerve ends. "That line about wanting your Edgar back." Nick's voice was casual, as if the question held little interest for him. "Was that just an excuse to come here?"

"I wanted to see you, and apologize. Set the record straight. I admit that." She was rewarded with a smile playing across the corners of his mouth. Faith reached up and touched him, her fingers soft against his lips. "But I do want the Edgar back. When I tell Prue I'm leaving the Foundation—"

Nick was stunned. "You're what?"

"I'm going to write full-time. I won't be happy until I try."

He grinned at her. "Congratulations."

"Better late than never. Anyway, I want to have the

Edgar with me when I tell Prue. To remind me what's at stake, to not back down."

"Maybe you should take along a witness," Nick said playfully. "To prove you're Fanny Duvall. The Edgar is impressive, but you could have gotten it from a pawn-shop."

"Where would I get a witness?" she asked.

"Me." Nick's grin grew broader. "I'd love to film that scene, and I was always quite fond of Fanny Duvall."

Faith smiled wickedly. "No kidding."

His arms pulled her close. "I take it you're telling me to go ahead and kiss you?"

"Why, no, I—"

"Because I'm going to."

This time the kiss was the ravenous kind that had tormented Faith's memory. She parted her lips and met his tongue eagerly, surrendering to a pleasure she had feared would never be hers again.

Nick kissed her again and again, each kiss deeper and more fiery than the last. Somehow their positions shifted until she was sprawled on her back with Nick lying over her. Faith felt the evidence of his desire for her and a thrill of pride and anticipation ran over her body. Soon he would ask her to leave with him, and she would say yes.

Nick nuzzled her neck, his tongue darting in and out of her ear, his teeth gently nipping her earlobe. Faith arched toward him, purring with pleasure, her heart aching with how much she loved him. His hands moved to loosen the ties of her dress, and Faith gasped. If they didn't leave soon, he would take her here—

"Fanny." Nick's voice was as ragged as his breathing. "Sweet, I—"

There was a sudden, eerie silence. Faith, as she watched Nick's head silhouetted against the moonlit window, saw all the twinkling yellow lights vanish in a pool of black.

"Oh, God, no!" she cried.

Nick knew the same instant she did; he lifted his body from hers and jackknifed around to look out the window, seeking confirmation of what was already certain.

"Nick, the lights!" There was a hint of hysteria in Faith's voice. The lights, the million fabled lights of Manhattan, were gone.

"Shh," he whispered. "Maybe somebody kicked out a plug at Con Ed. They'll come back on in a moment or two." Nick tried clicking on the lamp switch, with no result.

Faith sat up and rested her head against Nick's shoulder. They sat very still for some minutes, waiting for the comforting hum of the air conditioner, each wondering what would happen if the sound never came. Then, sensing Faith's growing fear, Nick went into action.

"If we're stuck here, we might as well be as comfortable as possible," he said calmly.

The moonlight gave a faint, greyish illumination. Faith's eyes slowly adjusted. Nick disappeared out the door, only to reappear with a half-dozen candles of varying sizes and shapes. He anchored them in ashtrays, then set them strategically around until the room gleamed like a Byzantine shrine.

"What do you say? Shall we raid the refrigerator before all the goodies spoil?"

"Refrigerator?" Then Faith saw it, a tiny square cubicle against the wall.

"Come on, it would be criminal to waste this," Nick urged, so they feasted on shrimp, and green grapes and mandarin oranges, and champagne and ice cream.

There seemed to be no time in this mysteriously stopped world, only Nick and his nearness and her happiness. Faith stared at Nick as he lounged on the sofa, hair tousled, shirt half-open and sleeves rolled up, a glass of champagne in his long fingers adding a touch of rakish elegance. She wanted to seal this moment in her memory. The candlelight softened the hard planes of his face, mellowing him; he looked hot, exhausted and endearingly boyish. Faith had never found him so captivating.

A smile curved about her lips as she looked at him with undisguised emotion. Nick caught her glance and smiled back, a provocative, adult-to-adult smile that showed he had read her thoughts.

He set down the champagne glass and Faith held out her arms to him. "Ah, Fanny . . ."

Nick covered her with kisses, her forehead and eyelids and cheekbones and jaw, until Faith thought she would dissolve under his lips into a vapor.

Faith called his name and it was a wild sound. She saw green fires, the reflection of candle flames dancing in his eyes. Her lips parted and he took them with an impatient hunger that stole her breath away.

"Nick! We can't—here—"

"Why not?" he demanded sensibly, and devastated her throat with a series of nibbling kisses. "Don't you believe in fate?"

"Yes," she moaned.

"Well, fate is keeping us prisoner here, and I say make the best of it."

"Oh, you're the best all right," Faith whispered. She was achingly disappointed when, out of nowhere, the power returned and the lamp snapped on, breaking the mood.

"Damn," Nick hissed, as Faith struggled up to a sitting position.

"So much for fate," she said lightly. "I guess I'd better go—"

"Don't you dare." With one strong snap of his wrist Nick extinguished the light, returning the room to its rutilant glow.

Faith gasped, and gasped again as his hands found

their way down the sensitive column of her bare back. "No—"

But against her will her hand slipped inside the open front of his shirt, felt the firm lines of his ribs. "No. Darling—"

Nick's mouth caught hers then, wiping out her words, wiping out any thought beyond this room and his touch and his need for her. Faith had thought she knew his style, his passion, but this! This was elemental, primitive, something that poured from the very core of his being.

Nick reached behind her neck to untie the fastening of her halter dress, and his fingers were trembling. Somehow this electrified her more than any practiced, confident caress could have. Nick drew her bodice down, his hands seeking her breasts, his fingers flicking across her already hardened nipples. Faith caught her breath as new desire coursed through her, something hard and demanding and entirely wanton. She found herself drawing Nick's head down to her swollen breasts.

"Kiss me," she begged, and when he did she seemed to burst into flames. Nick tugged her dress off, urgently, his hands sliding under her bottom and molding her to him. The feeling of his skin, hot and rough against her softness, set off a throbbing deep in her pelvis that drove her ever closer against him.

"Oh, God," she moaned, and felt the steel of his belt buckle digging into her skin. Impatiently she dealt with the fastening of his belt, reached for the tab of his zipper. She felt him then, hard and urgent under her hand. She froze in shock.

Nick lifted his head from the lazy exploration of her breasts. "Go on, Fanny. Don't stop now."

Her hand began to shake. Faith gulped and then, willing to do anything to please him, overcame her inhibitions. She pulled the tab down, her eyes closed, her hands somehow sliding the fabric down his body. With

an impatient grace Nick shrugged his way out of the rest
of his clothes, as if he couldn't be bothered with their
existence, his body aroused and gleaming in the candlelight. He stared down at Faith with a mesmerizing
intensity; she felt herself grow faint as she recognized the
yearning in his eyes.

"You are so pretty," he whispered shakily, and for the
first time in her life Faith believed it to be so. He touched
the side of her face with inexpressible tenderness.

Faith remembered, then, that Nick liked her hair down,
and she reached up for the ribbon and pins anchoring
her Gibson. She pulled out the pins, one by one, shaking
her hair down about her shoulders in slow, sensuous
movements.

She read his appreciation deep in his eyes, felt it as,
seeking to please her, he traced erotic patterns along the
soft flesh of her inner thigh. His hands snaked upward
and stroked maddeningly until Faith was aroused to such
a fever she could do nothing but toss from side to side
and moan in ecstasy.

Faith reached for him and drew him down on top of
her. She felt Nick's hard length pressing into her, insis-
tent, demanding. She tried to fit the curves of her body
into his.

"Fanny." Nick's voice left no doubt of his passion. "I
can't wait. I need you so much—"

"Then make love to me," she whispered.
"Please . . ."

A moan broke from him, an animal sound, and Faith
forgot everything but her need to feel him inside her.
Soon. Now.

Nick took her with such force she could only cling
dizzily to him and feel her body rock in its own maddening rhythm. He poured himself into her with an envelop-
ing, selfless attention to her own pleasure that left Faith's

senses devastated and her body drained and utterly spent.

Faith wondered, afterward, how Nick could still have the strength to hold her so tightly, when she barely had the energy left to breathe. He wound his hand in her hair and smiled down at her.

"Your eyes are green," she murmured idiotically. Faith wondered if she would ever tire of watching the swirling specks of color in the mysterious depths of his eyes.

"And you"—he laid a finger tenderly on her lower lip—"have the sweetest, softest lips in the whole world." He kissed her gently once, then again.

"I love you." The words flowed out of Faith without her willing them.

Nick's body stiffened instantly. "Don't say that."

"Why not?"

"You don't mean it." There was a note of sorrow behind his matter-of-fact voice. "One of us will get hurt."

"How dare you say that?" Faith demanded, hurt already. "I don't run around saying 'I love you' to every man I meet, you know. I think I know whether or not I meant it."

"Fanny, you don't know what you want."

"How can you say that?" she asked angrily. "After all—"

"Look, you just broke your engagement," he replied, maddeningly calm. "You're probably on the rebound. You're certainly in no state to be making declarations of undying love. Not yet."

Faith sat up and began pulling on her clothes. "I'll state anything I damn please, Mr. Justin. And if you don't like it—"

"You'll what?" There was a glint almost of merriment in Nick's eyes, but Faith didn't see it. The full skirt of her dress was over her head, and her mind was fully occupied trying to decipher the strange sounds coming from the hallway. If one of Nick's colleagues were to walk in on them. . . .

She picked up Nick's trousers and flung them at him in a ball. "Put these on," she said urgently as the sounds drew closer.

"Why?" He was almost laughing at her discomfiture.

"Oh, it's all very well for you to carry on your love affairs wherever you please, Mr. Justin, but I have a reputation to think of."

He pulled the pants on obediently, then leaned across to help Faith tie the bodice of her dress. "Must protect the lady's reputation at all costs—" he began teasingly as he pulled Faith back against him.

The door flew open and, as they whirled around, a voice spoke from the suddenly open doorway.

"It's a bit late for that, wouldn't you say?"

10

Faith knew who was there without having to lift her eyes. She heard the quick hiss of Nick's breath and realized, as his hands turned to iron at the nape of her neck, that he also recognized that sepulchral voice.

"Aunt Prue!" Faith turned ashen. Then, as her aunt's eyes swept the room from the disarranged sofa pillows to the candles to the cast-aside white straw sandals, Faith's cheeks began to burn.

"What are you doing here, Miss Daniels?" Nick's voice was cold and Faith wondered how he could summon such deadly calm when she was shaking.

When Prue did not answer, Nick turned his attention to the other figure in the doorway, a grey-uniformed security guard. "Mickey? How'd she get up here?"

"She made me bring her up, Mr. Justin," the tall man whined. "Said her niece was missing—"

"Missing!" Faith cried out. "But that's ridiculous!"

"There was a blackout—if you were in any condition

175

to notice it." Prue's crisp voice was both angry and defensive. "I was worried about you. When I called Bonnie and found out you weren't at home, I was naturally concerned."

"And Bonnie told you I'd come here." Faith phrased it as a statement, not a question. "So you had to come snooping around."

"I had good cause," Prue insisted. "After what Harald said about you and Nick Justin. . . ." She paused, her eyes sweeping the room. "And he was right! The minute I turn my back, what do I find but you running to the arms of your lover!"

Faith gasped. "My lover!" There was no way she could claim Nick as her lover; that had such a ring of commitment, of permanence to it, that she felt presumptuous using the word.

Nick interrupted Faith's protestations with a lazy drawl. "If you've come to ask my intentions—"

"I know your intentions," Prue retorted, "and you should be good and ashamed of them."

"You don't give either of us much credit," Nick said quietly, danger beginning to blaze in his hazel eyes.

"Oh, come now, Mr. Justin, what could you possibly want with a perfectly ordinary girl like Faith, except a roll in the hay?"

"Aunt Prue!" Faith nearly screamed with mortification. Prue was probably right, but it was horrible to hear, especially at this time and in this company. "Please, let's not discuss this."

"Oh, but we should," Nick said smoothly. "In the first place, Faith is not a girl. She's a woman. And while she may be perfect"—he flashed his quick, warm smile— "she's hardly ordinary. In fact, for quite a while now I've been forced to consider Faith one of the most remarkable women I've ever known."

Faith caught her breath, too stunned to speak. If only Nick's words were prompted by something other than the desire to overrule her aunt! But Faith was only too familiar with the way Prue could bring out one's perversity, making one disagree just for the sake of argument.

And it was torture to hear Nick praise her without really meaning it.

"I'm not interested in her performance in bed," Prue snapped. Then she sighed. "Poor Harald. No wonder he broke the engagement—"

"He broke the engagement!" Faith cried. "Is that what he told you? After I practically had to stuff his damn ring down his throat to get him to take it back—"

"Oh, Faith." Prue clucked sadly, as if Faith were breaking Commandments right in front of her. "You were cheating on the man, you got caught, he broke it off—why compound your failings by lying?"

"I broke the engagement because I didn't want to marry Harald. Period." Faith tried to sound convincing, but her voice shook with anger. "I only said yes in the first place because I wanted to make you happy—"

Prue laughed harshly. "As if you ever thought of me—"

"Yes! To make you happy! Because I wanted to get married and because Harald was the only man you approved of."

"And I suppose his money and his family meant nothing to you," Prue shot back.

"They meant a lot more to you than they did to me," Faith retorted. "I just wanted a chance for a halfway normal life with a man who loved me. And then . . ."

Then what? She met Nick Justin and fell in love and suddenly the "halfway normal life" was no longer enough, the "acceptable" fiancé intolerable.

But when Faith saw the stony censure in her aunt's

eyes, she despaired of ever finding the right words to explain herself. And Nick, taut as a panther behind her, made everything worse.

"You needn't explain," Prue said, her voice cold. "I can see very well what happened. Spare me the details of your cheap affair."

Suddenly her voice snapped. "My God, Faith! You are a Daniels! How could you disgrace us like this?"

"Now hold on a second, lady," Nick said, and his eyes smoked with anger. "I won't stand here and listen to Faith being abused—I don't care who you are. You'd better leave before I throw you out."

"Then Faith is coming with me," Prue said firmly. "And you can be sure I'll put a stop to this—this alley-cat behavior—at once. Come along, Faith."

"No." Faith's voice rang out like a bell. "I'm not a baby to be summoned. I admit I've hidden things from you, Aunt Prue, because I loved you and I wanted to shield you—"

"Bah," Prue said.

"That's true. I also admit I've been afraid to tell you the truth. But since you say you want an explanation, fine. Here goes.

"My relationship with Mr. Justin is purely business." Faith saw something painful flick across Nick's face, but she steeled herself and went on.

"Business!" Prue snorted, and wrinkled her nose in disbelief.

"Yes. Mr. Justin is doing a story on me. That's the full extent of his interest."

"Don't talk nonsense, child. What could *Newsview* possibly want with a story on you?"

Prue frowned and turned her attention to Nick. "If you were interested in a story on the Daniels Foundation, Mr. Justin, you should have come directly to me. And if, as I suspect, you were merely using that line to seduce this child—"

Faith saw the rage gathering on Nick's face and spoke quickly to avert the explosion. "Quite the opposite, Auntie. In fact, Nick thought I was trying to seduce him."

Nick flushed and Faith felt color spread over her own cheeks. "That wasn't true, not in the sense that he meant it, but maybe Nick wasn't entirely wrong. You see, I was afraid to have Nick's story go on the air, because he wanted to talk primarily about my book."

"Your . . . book?" Prue repeated dumbfoundedly, as if Faith had suddenly begun to speak a foreign language.

"Yes. I wrote a book called *Blood Poisoning.* A murder mystery. I don't think you'll like it much," Faith said frankly.

"My God. A *murder* mystery."

"Oh, don't look so worried, Auntie, I didn't soil the family name," Faith continued impatiently. "I used a pseudonym. But I made a mistake—"

"It would seem you made many," Prue retorted.

"I was nominated for an award and I went—like a fool—and I won and Nick was there and ever since I've been trying to convince him not to do a story about me. And failing," Faith finished in a rush.

"I see." Prue sighed. "Well at least you've gotten this madness out of your system."

"No!" Faith's chin lifted defiantly. "Don't you understand? I'm proud of *Blood Poisoning,* prouder of it than anything I've ever done."

"Oh, really? Then why hide the fact that you wrote it?"

"I didn't want to hurt you," Faith whispered.

"Well, you have hurt me. Hurt me dreadfully. How can I ever hold my head up in this town, after your—your trashy book and your scandalous conduct?"

Prue paused, then gathered herself together with an

effort and seized Faith's arm. "Well, there'll be no more of these wild oats, young lady. You're coming home right now. Mr. Justin will cancel his story—if indeed there ever was one—and there'll be no more books. If you want to write we'll find plenty to keep you busy at the Foundation." She turned briskly toward the door.

"Damn the Foundation," Faith muttered and stood where she was.

Prue gasped. "What did you say?"

"You heard me. I'm leaving the Foundation. Effective immediately. I'm going to write full-time. And I'll write what I choose—"

"You can't do that!" Prue bellowed.

"Oh, yes I can. You'll do fine without me. I can recommend some excellent candidates for my job—"

"Faith, you are a Daniels! The Foundation has to come first! Think of your father!"

"And what about her talent?" Nick asked angrily. "What about her hopes and dreams?"

"What about family? Loyalty? Dedication? Selflessness?" Prue shot back. "How could you even consider abandoning your father's noble dream to write—what is it? Murder mysteries? My God, Faith! Poor Harrison must be turning in his grave!"

"I'm sure he is," Faith said quietly, "but not because of me."

Prue drew herself up, straight and steely. "You can't pretend that he would object to me trying to carry on his life's work—"

"My father's life's work was to help people be free," Faith responded firmly. "The last thing he'd ever want is for his dream to make me a slave."

And having finally said what she'd needed to say for years, Faith strode out of the room.

* * *

Sunset came softly the next evening. Tendrils of rose and lavender wrapped the skyline of Manhattan in a gentle embrace. Faith found herself in the gazebo, Figaro by her side, the ever-present pad and pen in her lap.

She had gone to the Foundation and cleaned out her desk; Prue had studiously avoided her as if she had the plague.

And she hadn't heard a word from Nick Justin.

Ah well, Faith thought. It had been wonderful while it lasted, wonderful to hear him defending her even if he did it from sheer gallantry. Wonderful to pretend that there might be something more than a casual fling between them.

But if there weren't. . . .

Faith bit her lip and forced herself to face facts. She loved Nick Justin to the very root of her being, but if he didn't love her in return—and why should he, really?— her life was infinitely richer for his having passed through it. Faith could not regret, for one instant, loving him. And she must be greedy to want anything more.

Faith hugged Figaro and watched the sky turn slowly from pale blue to indigo. Squirrels scampered among the trees, frogs croaked, the water slapped rhythmically against the bank.

A foreign sound pierced the stillness. Creak. Creak. Faith tensed. Her fingers twined around the whistle she always wore in the park. But the sound did not harken danger, simply a note out of place.

Creak. There it was again. A picture swam through Faith's head and she recognized the sound: an oar creaking in an oarlock. Someone was rowing across the pond.

A quiver ran along Faith's veins. She knew all the boats were chained up behind a chain-link fence. Whoever was on the pond now had surely broken the law and taken the boat. An innocent kind of mischief, but illegal nonetheless.

Faith smiled. Now who could crave some moments in a rowboat so desperately that he or she would risk arrest to have them? An exercise freak, who had missed his daily workout? Teenagers, out to test their ingenuity against the fence? Or lovers, drawn to the lake in the evening?

At this last, a twist of pain shot through Faith's heart. Lovers, most likely. And she was in no mood to watch someone else's courtship. Not this evening.

Faith had stored her notebook in her purse and prepared to leave when the shape of the boat came into view. Faith squinted at the far-off hull. Not lovers. A solitary rower.

She sat down again, heavily, the bench suddenly hard and unyielding beneath her. Faith watched the rhythmic sweep of arms and shoulders as if hypnotized. The silhouette was hauntingly familiar.

"No, it can't be," she murmured aloud in panic. But she could not move. The boat came closer, straight for the dock at the foot of the gazebo. Faith's heart accelerated. The figure paused and passed a hand carelessly across his brow, as if to brush hair out of his eyes.

Nick Justin.

Faith knew it was him, long before the boat pulled up at her feet. He had come for her, and had stolen a boat to do so. His reporter's instincts had told him just where she'd be.

"Hello, Fanny," he called softly. "Can we talk?"

"In that?" She was incredulous.

"Why not?" His voice coaxed her. "Bring Figaro."

Against her better judgment, Faith climbed into the rowboat, carefully arranging her fragile pink dress on the damp wood. "How did you find me?" she asked shakily.

"Instinct." She felt, rather than saw, his smile. Nick dipped the oars and pushed off; they moved in silence for some minutes. The time seemed eternal to Faith's over-wrought nerves.

At last Nick lifted his head. "Fanny, we have to talk. We have to set things straight between us."

"No, we don't." Now he would explain that their relationship was simply casual as far as he was con-cerned, and she didn't want to hear him say that he didn't love her. "You don't have to say anything." Her voice was frantic.

"But you have to know how I feel. You have a right." He paused and swallowed, as if speech were difficult. "Fanny—"

"Please, Nick, just let it go. We're friends now, aren't we?"

"Are we?" His dark gaze was disturbing. "After the way you walked out yesterday—and you haven't been answering your phone—"

"I'm sorry. I needed to be alone."

"I see." The oars dipped. Faith trailed her hand absently in the water, studying his strong hands knotted around the wooden oars, the moonlight silvering his hair.

"I've said that, too," he remarked quietly. "That I needed to be alone. After Cynthia . . ." He paused. "I insulated myself. I made up my mind I would never get hurt again."

Faith recognized where the conversation was going. Now he would explain why he couldn't make a commit-ment to her.

"It worked, too," he said roughly. "Worked damn well. I had myself convinced that the all-consuming desire to possess a woman, body and soul, happened only once in a lifetime, and only to the young. I was safe. I was immune."

The oars dipped violently, the boat sprang forward.

"And then I walked into a ballroom and saw this woman. Just a girl, really, and not my type at all—too tall and too skinny and more sweet than spicy. But I looked in her eyes and my heart dropped down to my knees and I thought, 'Oh, hell, no. Not twice in one lifetime.'"

Faith's heart began to beat wildly. She pressed her fingers to her open mouth.

"I treated you abominably, I know," Nick said softly. "But you were with Ken Powell, and I knew Powell was married; I knew the kind of woman you had to be. I despised myself for being so vulnerable as to be attracted to you. To want you, no matter what. That tormented me, and so I tormented you."

"I'll say you did," Faith said ruefully.

"Poor Fanny," Nick said. "What you must have thought—"

"I thought you were insufferable and the most arrogant man on earth. And I was terrified of you. You seemed to hate me so. . . ."

"Do you wonder why?" Nick asked. "I was sure you were the same kind of witch Cynthia was. You and Powell were so intimate—"

"Intimate!" And Faith told him how she'd met Ken.

Nick groaned. "So that's all there was to it? When I saw you in Powell's arms I wanted to kill him. And when you ran out of the ballroom, and I realized that I might never see you again—"

He stopped.

"You laid a trap for me, didn't you? With the cabs."

He nodded. "It was obvious you intended to run away. I thought if I investigated you, that would snap me out of my infatuation. There had to be some ugly reality under those secrets of yours. I thought if I found it out, I wouldn't want you."

He smiled ruefully. "But I couldn't keep my hands off you, even in the cab. I was so rotten to you, Fanny, how could you ever forgive me?"

"I forgave you long ago," Faith said softly.

He continued as if she hadn't spoken. "It was so plain that you were lying! The more I probed, the worse it looked. You had to be a fraud, a cheat—yet the more I was with you the more I wanted you."

He shook his head. "I thought I'd done it again, you see. Fallen for a woman with no scruples and no heart."

"I wanted to tell you the truth, almost from the beginning," Faith confessed. "I nearly told you in the cab."

"If only you had!"

"I was afraid to. You'd be kind and gentle for a moment, and then you'd be so forbidding. I couldn't trust a man who seemed to hate me so."

"Hate you!" Nick groaned again. "When I lost you on the subway platform in Harlem—"

"You looked like you wanted to murder me."

"I had realized that I didn't even know your name. That I might never find you again. That was the worst part, believe me." Nick brushed his hair out of his eyes. "But it also scared me, even more. After I rescued you—well, I thought you trusted me by then. And if you needed to run from the police, well, you had to be hiding something criminal."

The oars creaked. "Thank God for Mildred, or I might never have found you."

"Nick, when you heard my story," Faith ventured slowly, "well, you were all geared up for bigamy or bank robbery or something spectacular. When the truth turned out to be that I was just a scared little kid . . ." She swallowed. "Well, what did you think of me?"

Nick's eyes met hers; their expression took her breath

away. "Oh, Fanny. I wanted to put my arms around you and hold you tight and tell you that no one would ever hurt you again."

"Well, why the hell didn't you?" she demanded.

"How could I? You were with your fiancé and you hated the sight of me."

"Never," Faith declared. "I thought *you* hated *me.* You gave a pretty good impression of it."

He let the oars go then. The boat drifted in the open water as Nick's hands reached across for Faith's and held them tightly.

"You must have thought me a terrible baby." Faith sighed.

Nick smiled. "You're nobody's baby anymore, kid. Have I told you how proud I was to see you march out of my office yesterday?"

"No." Faith grinned. "Tell me."

He grinned back, his eyes shot with silver in the moonlight. "You were wonderful. I loved you more than ever."

"You—what?" Faith felt as if all the oxygen in the universe had suddenly evaporated.

"I loved you," Nick repeated, with a tremor deep in his voice. "Always have, still do, always will. Any questions?"

Faith saw behind the brevity to the fountain of passion only precariously restrained, which threatened to explode and drown them both.

"But last night you wouldn't let me say I loved you," she protested.

"I was afraid to hear it," Nick admitted softly. "Afraid you didn't mean it, that my heart would break again when you left me. You were always running away from me," he added accusingly.

Faith let herself be pulled across the boat into his arms. "Never again," she vowed passionately. "Darling . . ."

They kissed with the full force of their newly awakened passion, and the boat rocked dangerously for several minutes. At last Faith sank down into Nick's lap, blissfully exhausted, her smile so wide her mouth ached.

"What now?" she asked drowsily.

"Now," he replied, in a voice husky with passion, "I'm going to take you home and make love to you for about two weeks, unless"—he paused and grinned wickedly—"you want to be alone."

"No way," Faith said, snuggling close.

"Are you sure?" Nick's hand slid possessively over her breast and sent a shiver through her. "After all, you've never lived alone, been independent. Maybe you need that. And if you do, I want you to go ahead and do it. I'll wait for you. However long you need—"

Faith thought she had never seen his rugged face so vulnerable. She laid a finger against his lips and spoke quickly to take him out of his misery.

"Don't tell me what I want, Mr. Justin. I can think for myself, remember?"

"Yes, ma'am." He grinned down at her. "You know, Fanny, I'm no prize package. I have a child and a high-pressure career and, I'm told, a hell of a temper—"

"Well, don't pussyfoot around," Faith teased. "Give it to me straight."

Nick pulled her close. "I love you more than anything else in the world. But that's no reason to marry me. Because you'll always have my love, whether we're together or apart—and frankly, Fanny, I think you could do a lot better."

"No doubt," she said, as if her heart weren't turning cartwheels. "But I have this little problem. I happen to love you. You and only you."

She lifted her lips to his and kissed him in a way that left no doubt of her feelings. Nick groaned and slid his hands possessively over her.

"And if those famous reporter's instincts of yours haven't told you by now that we're meant for each other—"

"Does that mean," Nick was breathless, "that you'll take a chance and marry me?"

"For better or worse, I will," Faith said. "And the sooner the better."

A smile with the force of sunlight broke across Nick Justin's face.

"You'll never regret it, sweetheart," said Faith's husband-to-be, with a creditable imitation of Humphrey Bogart.

And she never did.

Enjoy love and passion, larger than life!

Let new Silhouette Intimate Moments romance novels take you to the world of your dreams ...and beyond.

Try them for 15 days, free.

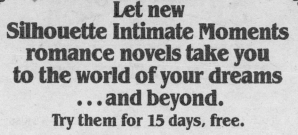

Our new series, Silhouette Intimate Moments, is so full of love and excitement, you won't be able to put these books down. We've developed these books for a special kind of reader—one who isn't afraid to be swept away by passion and adventure.

The characters lead thrilling lives—and their feelings are as real and intimate as yours. So you'll share all the joys and sorrows of each heroine.

Enjoy 4 books, free, for 15 days...

When you mail this coupon, we'll send you 4 Silhouette Intimate Moments novels to look over for 15 days. If you're not delighted, simply return them and owe nothing. But if you enjoy them as much as we think you will, just pay the invoice, and we'll send you 4 books each month, as soon as they are published. And there's never a charge for postage or handling!

Mail the coupon below right now. And soon you'll read novels that capture your imagination and carry you away to the world you've always dreamed of!

YOU'LL BE SWEPT AWAY
WITH SILHOUETTE DESIRE

$1.75 each

1 ☐ CORPORATE AFFAIR
James

2 ☐ LOVE'S SILVER WEB
Monet

3 ☐ WISE FOLLY
Clay

4 ☐ KISS AND TELL
Carey

5 ☐ WHEN LAST WE LOVED
Baker

6 ☐ A FRENCHMAN'S KISS
Mallory

7 ☐ NOT EVEN FOR LOVE
St. Claire

8 ☐ MAKE NO PROMISES
Dee

9 ☐ MOMENT IN TIME
Simms

10 ☐ WHENEVER I LOVE YOU
Smith

$1.95 each

11 ☐ VELVET TOUCH
James

12 ☐ THE COWBOY AND THE
LADY   Palmer

13 ☐ COME BACK, MY LOVE
Wallace

14 ☐ BLANKET OF STARS
Valley

15 ☐ SWEET BONDAGE
Vernon

16 ☐ DREAM COME TRUE
Major

19 ☐ LOVER IN PURSUIT
James

20 ☐ KING OF DIAMONDS
Allison

21 ☐ LOVE IN THE CHINA SEA
Baker

22 ☐ BITTERSWEET IN BERN
Durant

23 ☐ CONSTANT STRANGER
Sunshine

24 ☐ SHARED MOMENTS
Baxter

25 ☐ RENAISSANCE MAN
James

26 ☐ SEPTEMBER MORNING
Palmer

27 ☐ ON WINGS OF NIGHT
Conrad

28 ☐ PASSIONATE JOURNEY
Lovan

29 ☐ ENCHANTED DESERT
Michelle

30 ☐ PAST FORGETTING
Lind

31 ☐ RECKLESS PASSION
James

32 ☐ YESTERDAY'S DREAMS
Clay

38 ☐ SWEET SERENITY
Douglass

39 ☐ SHADOW OF BETRAYAL
Monet

40 ☐ GENTLE CONQUEST
Mallory

41 ☐ SEDUCTION BY DESIGN
St. Claire

Silhouette Desire

42 ☐ ASK ME NO SECRETS
Stewart

43 ☐ A WILD, SWEET MAGIC
Simms

44 ☐ HEART OVER MIND West

45 ☐ EXPERIMENT IN LOVE Clay

46 ☐ HER GOLDEN EYES Chance

47 ☐ SILVER PROMISES Michelle

48 ☐ DREAM OF THE WEST
Powers

49 ☐ AFFAIR OF HONOR James

50 ☐ FRIENDS AND LOVERS
Palmer

51 ☐ SHADOW OF THE
MOUNTAIN Lind

52 ☐ EMBERS OF THE SUN
Morgan

53 ☐ WINTER LADY Joyce

54 ☐ IF EVER YOU NEED ME
Fulford

55 ☐ TO TAME THE HUNTER
James

56 ☐ FLIP SIDE OF YESTERDAY
Douglass

57 ☐ NO PLACE FOR A WOMAN
Michelle

58 ☐ ONE NIGHT'S DECEPTION
Mallory

59 ☐ TIME STANDS STILL
Powers

60 ☐ BETWEEN THE LINES
Dennis

61 ☐ ALL THE NIGHT LONG
Simms

62 ☐ PASSIONATE SILENCE
Monet

63 ☐ SHARE YOUR
TOMORROWS Dee

64 ☐ SONATINA
Milan

65 ☐ RECKLESS VENTURE
Allison

66 ☐ THE FIERCE GENTLENESS
Langtry

67 ☐ GAMEMASTER
James

68 ☐ SHADOW OF YESTERDAY
Browning

69 ☐ PASSION'S PORTRAIT
Carey

70 ☐ DINNER FOR TWO
Victor

71 ☐ MAN OF THE HOUSE
Joyce

72 ☐ NOBODY'S BABY
Hart

SILHOUETTE DESIRE, Department SD/6
1230 Avenue of the Americas
New York, NY 10020

Please send me the books I have checked above. I am enclosing $_____
(please add 50¢ to cover postage and handling. NYS and NYC residents please add appropriate sales tax.) Send check or money order—no cash or C.O.D.'s please. Allow six weeks for delivery.

NAME _____

ADDRESS _____

CITY _____ STATE/ZIP _____